SENTENCED TO FREEDOM

FROM IRON BARS TO PEARL GATES

BRYCE RUNTE

Published by
Innovo Publishing, LLC
www.innovopublishing.com
1-888-546-2111

Providing Full-Service Publishing Services for
Christian Authors, Artists & Organizations: Hardbacks, Paperbacks,
eBooks, Audiobooks, Music & Film

SENTENCED TO FREEDOM: FROM IRON BARS TO PEARL GATES

All Scripture references are from the American King James version of the
Bible, quoted from www.biblehub.com. Used by permission. All rights
reserved worldwide.

The characters and events portrayed in this book are fictitious. Any similarity
to a real person, living or dead, is coincidental and not intended by the author.

Library of Congress Control Number: 2016962941
ISBN: 978-1-61314-365-0

Cover Design & Interior Layout: Innovo Publishing, LLC

Printed in the United States of America
U.S. Printing History
First Edition: February 2017

ACKNOWLEDGEMENTS

First, I thank my Lord and Savior Jesus Christ for telling this story through me. I never envisioned writing as something you had for me, but here I am. Lord, I simply try to do what I know some songwriters to do, and that is just to take the story or song that you have already created and put it down on paper. Everything that comes from the publication of this book is all because of you and is all for you alone. May you use it according to your will.

I also would like to thank my family and friends for their support of the book during the writing and publishing stages. In one way or another you all have been a blessing and an encouragement to me and am very thankful to God for having you all with me during this walk of faith. I love you all very much.

Lastly I would like to thank Innovo Publishing for agreeing to publish this book and I am especially thankful for the patience they have shown and continue to show me as I grow in the industry. May the Lord bless and keep you in all that you do.

CHAPTER 1

If the city of Mobile, Alabama could be defined as anything, it would be accurate to say that it is delusional and divided. Most on the outside would look out and point out a number of things that could be the problem. One might point out the crime. "Crime may be present in our city," some would say, "but at least it's not as bad as Chicago or New York." While it may be true that Mobile's crime is not like Chicago or New York, it is certainly one of the worst cities in the state of Alabama. One might point out the race issue. "After all of these years, they still haven't learned to let go of their hate and racism." It's true that some still cling to racism, on both sides of the aisle, mind you, but even if a white or black person don't like each other, for the most part, they still try to get along for the sake of peace. Some even respect each other in the midst of it. Shocking.

These things and others may seem like the answer, but the delusion and division come from something far different than mere problems like race or minor city issues. The division was taking a new form, pitting the city against a very specific sect of people, and the delusion was causing the people of that sect to not see it happening in its grandest forms. Some recognized it in some things, but most didn't recognize the gravity of the issue. Who were the delusional people under attack from the city? They were the one group of people who, if they utilized the power that had been given them, could stand in the way of a grand scheme of corruption and chaos passed down over generations and down from the federal and state governments. Some of them sought to push back against the attacks, not in hatred but in truth and love, but there were too few of them willing to take the stand, and the ones that did had their lives sacked by government agencies of all levels. Some even went to prison, the same prison that held ruthless, depraved criminals. The same prison where the hatred from different cultures and backgrounds would culminate and there was no escaping it. The same prison where young guys like LaMarcus would go because their minds had been poisoned to live their life for the rep, the rush, the hood, the gang, whatever lie had been fed to them, that they craved.

And LaMarcus, though he had no desire to be in prison, wasn't going to back down either. He wasn't ashamed of what he did to get here, but now that he was here, he would toughen up and do what he had to do to survive. He knew if he could survive this, it would be a great experience for when he got back on the street. He had committed crimes before, but this was his first offense as an adult. Luckily some of the boys from his hood were locked up with him so he had a few allies to turn to in case things got ugly.

As for LaMarcus himself, he was only twenty years old. He was tall, rather skinny, but he could hold his own in a fight. In fact a week prior to his arrest, he had gotten in a fight over some dirty play in the basketball game with his buddies. He fought one of his best friends and made him bleed from his nose. Ironically not long after that fight they were laughing as if it never happened. The boys in LaMarcus's hood were all fairly close and had a rule: You could fight one another, but you couldn't use guns and you couldn't kill. You could only kill people from other hoods and it was only in defense of yourself or your brothers. It was because of this rule that made LaMarcus's gang look weak in comparison to the other notorious gangs of the city, but it was a rule that had been handed down from their parents all the way back to the days of Dr. King. Though LaMarcus would never admit it, he was glad this rule was in place because he like everyone else didn't want to see people killed. That having been said, if he had to do it, he would.

LaMarcus had a dark past and whether he realized it or not, he was using his gang involvement to escape that past. Survival was the excuse that he and the gang would preach over and over again in defense of their actions to anyone who questioned them. Even his own mother once told him, "You're not solving any problems by running around and acting like a hoodlum." LaMarcus, however, was involved for a number of reasons. For one, he felt like it was his duty to live "the life" with his friends. He disagreed with his mother and believed that he was solving the problems of his life. They didn't have money for something, so he'd go and take it. Whenever he felt disrespected, he beat it out of whoever he needed to. No matter the situation, he would use everything that was buried in him and unleash it on whoever dared cross his path. It was the only way he knew how to deal with his anger and it was the very reason his mother was afraid for him.

The other guys would look at him whenever he got a little too "into it" and just think to themselves, "he's just trying to live up to the family name," or most often, "it's like he's on a mission or something." What the other members didn't know was that LaMarcus would get this way after he'd have talks with his little brother, who thought that LaMarcus doing gang stuff was stupid. Every now and then his brother would say something that would cause him to begin to question if living a gang life was a real life worth living for. In other words, was this what he wanted or was this simply the only thing he knew to be real? Paranoid that the others would suspect weakness, LaMarcus would act out intensely so his loyalty would not be questioned. It's what got him arrested this particular night.

He thought about all of this as he was brought into the station for his booking. He put on his best behavior as he taunted and jeered at the cops the entire time. No, seriously, this was his best behavior. Anything worse and he may have had additional charges brought on him. LaMarcus welcomed the idea of getting tough in prison, but he didn't want to be there forever. He constantly kept pressing the cops with things like, "I see how it is. Y'all only want to get me 'cause I'm black. Y'all don't care about the white boys doing the same thing couple blocks over. Naw, y'all just want to be hatin' on me 'cause y'all are racist mother—"

"That's enough," said one officer present for the booking. "No more talking unless we ask you a question."

"Hey, whatever, man. I just know that this is some bull. I haven't done nothing to any one of y'all." LaMarcus was lying out of his teeth of course, but the officers knew it.

"We have evidence that links you to an armed robbery, a carjacking, and possession of stolen goods. Looking at your juvie record here, I'm surprised it took you this long to end up in an adult prison," said the other officer whose last name was Griffin. "Look at you. You're a young man throwing his life away when you do things like this. You're not like the others I see come through here. They come here without a care in the world. You come in here like you got something to prove. Why are you doing this to yourself?"

"What do you care?" LaMarcus snapped back, "You don't know me. You don't know what it's like to be in my world. I have to do what I can to survive. None of the rest of this world cares about me except my boys back in the hood. So I gotta do what's right for them and what's right for me. I'ma do me!"

Officer Griffin paused for a moment before he answered. "You're not doing your boys or yourself any favors by getting involved in stuff like this." From then on he didn't ask LaMarcus any more personal questions, only ones necessary for the booking. When he was finished he looked at his partner and said, "Officer Carter, would you take him down to get his mug shot please? I need some coffee." And so LaMarcus was taken to receive his mug shot and from there was placed in a holding cell with several other inmates.

"You'll be here for a couple of days 'til we get your trial arranged. Then we'll move you to the regular jail cells," said Officer Carter to LaMarcus. To the rest of the inmates he said, "Y'all have a new friend tonight. I better not hear of any stupid things happening in here. Ya got that?" The rest of the inmates just grunted at him and Officer Carter nodded to the officer in charge of the cell as he shut the door.

LaMarcus waited all night for someone to try to mess with him. It was usually a custom, at least it was at the juvenile detention center. It happened to him and he participated in it to other new inmates. This night was different. Aside from a few stares, nobody came near him. LaMarcus wasn't quite sure what to think of it. Did they just not have an interest in hazing him? No, it seemed more than that. He could tell they wanted to by their eyes. Even so, they hesitated. Even when the guard temporarily stepped away, which he shouldn't have done, they looked like they were about to walk to LaMarcus, but something was drawing them back.

The next morning, he tried to shrug off the event of the previous night, but he couldn't seem to get it out of his mind. He knew deep down it wasn't anything physically intimidating about him. The guys who were staring him down were three times his size. After thinking about it for a while, the only conclusion he could come up with was that maybe they were just waiting for the right opportunity. For now, he decided to just count himself lucky he got through the first night.

LaMarcus's transfer to the metro jail from the precinct took longer than expected because plans had been made to make room for him with the release of one inmate who had just finished his time. He was forced to wait in the precinct for a whole week, something that is an extreme rarity. If he had known the metro jail had the room for him anyway, but waited for the release of this one prisoner, he would have been really confused. In reality there was a mess-up with the release of the one prisoner because someone got the order of "release for good behavior" lost in a shuffle of other papers and the chief of police ordered all prisoner movements be suspended until the order was found. A little extreme, maybe, but this is how it happened; and needless to say, whoever lost the order obviously got fired.

The courthouse hadn't quite set up LaMarcus's trial date yet, but the police department felt compelled to move him anyway having waited as long as he had. LaMarcus was quite relieved about it. Things had been getting weird in that group cell in the precinct. He couldn't believe that no one tried to haze him, not once. One guy who'd been in and out of prison his whole life even told him, "You must have an angel looking out for you. I've never seen men that size cower from anyone before." LaMarcus didn't understand what he meant by *cower*. If he had been paying attention, he would have seen it in their eyes. They wanted to haze him. They wanted to teach this new kid about prison. But as they were staring down LaMarcus it was as if something was standing in their way and they couldn't move.

LaMarcus didn't believe in angels or God for that matter. If God was real, the world would be a better place, wouldn't it? If God cared, then He would've stopped all of the bad things that had happened in

LaMarcus's life. He didn't pay much mind to what the man said about a guardian angel, but it would become a thought that would begin to linger. All along the bus ride to the metro jail it lingered. Even as the guards formed the ranks of the new inmates, he could hardly focus on what was going on because of what happened, or rather what had not happened in the precinct.

There was a decent sized group with LaMarcus. Counting him, there were about thirty new inmates. As custom, the warden liked to address the new inmates before the guards started handing out cell assignments. He was a middle-aged man with a good bit of his hair left. He wasn't skinny but he wasn't overly big either. LaMarcus knew right away that this guy had been through his share of fights and not all of them physical. He was pretty gruff in his voice. He had to be. Prisoners were getting harder and harder to control every year.

"My name is Paul Knight. I am the warden of this fine institution. What I'm going to talk to you about today is what your lives will be like as long as you are staying here with us. Due to limited space, every single one of you will be getting a new cellmate today. Your cellmates know exactly how they are to treat you and the consequences if they go against those rules. Now I will inform you of these same rules. You don't have to like your cellmates, but you will respect them. Fights will simply not be tolerated…and that goes for any inmate at all. Any reports of fighting will result in all parties involved being locked in solitary confinement for two weeks. If the fight is with your cellmate, you will receive a month of solitary confinement and will be moved to a new cell upon your release. I will not have gang wars in my prison. You want to kill each other, you do it when you're outside these walls. When you're in here, you're a prisoner with no right to decide what clothes you'll wear much less the right to kill anyone. When you're in here, you're more an animal than you are human. Unlike other prisons though, we offer you a small sliver of your humanity, and as such we will not confine you 24/7 to your cells. After all, animals need to be let out of their cages every once in a while."

His voice turned very cold when he said this.

"You will receive meals at breakfast and dinner. If you're in solitary, you get to choose one or the other. We will allow two hours a day aside from meal breaks, which are themselves an hour, where you can exercise or have recreational time. Enjoy those moments, gentlemen. They'll be the closest thing to freedom that you will experience in this prison. Now I understand some of you may be a bit claustrophobic and need to get out of your cell a little bit more. Well we do offer services for you to participate in that will allow you extra time out of your cells in which you'll be working for the prison. Only trouble is you may experience a lot of humiliation from your fellow inmates if you decide to sign up. If you're interested, just mention something to a guard and we'll look into getting you hooked up. Understand something, all of you, the rules you think you know don't apply in here. All of you played by your rules and that led you here. Most prisons aren't designed to break down their prisoners. Gentlemen, this is not one of those prisons. But, never let it be said that I'm not a fair man. If you promise to play by my rules, then I promise there won't be any trouble, and things will go much smoother for you. Is that understood?"

Everyone gave a slight nod.

"Captain, issue them their cells." The captain and a few sergeants were sitting behind a desk. The captain kept calling names one by one and each prisoner escorted by another guard would come up and receive their cell assignment. Then the guard would take them to their cell. There were enough guards for all of the new inmates so none had to come back. Everything was down to a science, almost like a business.

"Russell, LaMarcus," the captain said. LaMarcus got up and was escorted by a guard to the captain just like all the ones before him. The captain, not looking at LaMarcus but instead at his papers, said to him, "You will be in Block C, cell 7."

Immediately after he said this, the sergeants couldn't hold their composure anymore and started snickering. The captain reprimanded both of them with a quick "Enough!" Then he looked LaMarcus in the eye and said, "Welcome to Mobile Metro Jail." The guard then began to escort LaMarcus to his cell. On the way to the cell, his curiosity got the better of him and he just had to say what was on his mind.

"Hey, why were those two snickering? What's their problem?"

The guard responded very coldly. "Not that I have to tell you, but they were snickering at your cell assignment."

"My cell assignment? What does that have to do with anything?"

The guard just snickered to himself and said, "You'll find out for yourself real soon."

In no time at all they were at the cell and the guard began to unshackle him. There was another guard not too far off in case LaMarcus tried anything funny.

"Welcome to your new home. It's recreational time so your cellmate will be back momentarily. Have fun with that." He started laughing as he walked off.

Instead of making use of the recreational time, LaMarcus decided to just stay at the cell. He was tired anyway, and there would be plenty of time to look for the boys during the free time tomorrow. The cell wasn't big—just as any normal jail cell would be. It had two beds clamped to the floor, a small toilet sticking out of the wall, and in-between the two beds part of the concrete wall stuck out, almost like a shelf. Sitting on top of this shelf was a small, battery-powered radio that wasn't currently turned on. He also noticed a piece of paper on one of the beds. It had a message written on it that said, "Welcome to cell C-7. This is your bed. Don't mess with the radio and I'll be back in a bit." LaMarcus was a bit taken aback by the message of not to mess with the radio. This was his cell too. That meant if a radio was in the room, he should be able to use it too. He went over to the radio and looked to turn it on. As he was fiddling with the radio, he heard a voice behind him say, "Can I help you, boy?"

CHAPTER 2

I t wasn't a mean or harsh voice, but it was worn and yet somehow full of energy. LaMarcus turned around to see who was standing there. To his surprise, he did not find a big, hard-hearted inmate but rather a simple, old-looking white man. He was shorter than LaMarcus, though LaMarcus himself was pretty tall, and he had a well-kept shadow of a beard. Though he was old, he still had hints of color in his hair, but most of it was made gray from the years.

LaMarcus wasn't quite sure what to make of him. He couldn't tell what it was, but something was just off about this guy, but not in a bad way. There was an air or a vibe about him that told LaMarcus that even though he was supposed to be an inmate, he wasn't a threat or any danger. And this man clearly didn't have any fear of LaMarcus at all. LaMarcus thought to himself, "Well, he must have done something to get in here. Maybe he's mental, or a sex offender." But the more LaMarcus thought about how he didn't seem like a threat, the more it made him wonder why all the guards had snickered earlier.

The old man finally spoke up again. "Wait, wait. I got it. You must be my new cellmate."

LaMarcus was hesitant to speak. "Yeah. I just got here. I was just adjusting to the new environment."

"Oh, you'll have plenty of time to do that," the old man replied. "Ain't much else you can do. Um, I don't mean to be rude, but you can read, right?"

LaMarcus was a bit taken aback. "What?"

"Well, I did ask in my note not to mess with my radio. You see, it'd be such a shame if it got damaged."

"Well, why should you be the only one to use it. I have every right to use it too. This is my cell too."

"Son, inside these walls, you have no rights at all, save but one and that's your right to exist. And with some of these guards, they feel as though that should be taken away too, no matter what crime you committed. I went through a lot to get that radio. The guards don't bother trying to take it anymore. Even still, I don't like to take the chance of it getting ruined."

LaMarcus was really starting to steam now. "Man, that's some bull right there. I get the one guy with a radio and he don't want to give it up. That's just great."

The old man just stared at him. "Besides, even if I let you use it now, it wouldn't do you much good anyway."

"Why not?"

"Because, it's a battery powered radio. I save the radio for special occasions. And because I have people constantly trying to use it, I hid the batteries."

"Wow. Not only will you not let me use it, but you don't even use it all the time."

"I'm sorry to sound so selfish, but that radio is really special to me. It's one of the last things I have left. I've only ever asked for two things during my time here, and that's one of them. That's why the warden let me have it in the first place. It's my second-most valued possession. But if it means all that much to you, you can use it."

LaMarcus rolled his eyes. "I don't even care anymore, man. Keep your stupid radio. Call me *boy*. Don't want to give up a radio. Everything I'd expect from a racist."

"I'm really not a racist. Just a little overprotective of my radio."

LaMarcus turned away, trying to end the conversation.

"Look, kid. We're gonna be spending a lot of time together, and I don't want to start off on the wrong foot. What's your name?"

"What do you care?" LaMarcus snapped.

"I figure the only way we'll survive the next few years is to get to know each other now. What's your name?"

"LaMarcus." He was getting really irritated now.

"You got a last name, LaMarcus?"

LaMarcus started to growl. "Russell." After a minute, LaMarcus decided to humor the old man. "And do you got a name? You know, besides *racist?*"

"Oh, most everyone who ever called me by my first name ain't alive no more. And since you're too young to do that, you can just call me Mr. Curtis like everyone else does," the old man replied.

"Mr. Curtis. Yeah. I'll get right on that." LaMarcus said, snidely. And that was the end of that conversation.

They didn't speak much the next couple of days. The old man could see LaMarcus really wanted nothing to do with him. LaMarcus was more interested in finding his buddies from the hood. He finally managed to find them one day during rec time. Two black men who were shorter and a little heftier than LaMarcus were making a beeline toward him, both with smiles on their faces. One was named Thomas and the other Kelvin. LaMarcus recognized them immediately and got excited.

"Yo, man, who is this shady who checked himself into my jailhouse?" Kelvin asked with a big grin. Kelvin was the biggest clown of the gang back home.

"Hey, dawg, what's happnin'?" LaMarcus answered as he hand-slapped both of them.

"Man, when'd you get sent up in here?" Thomas asked.

"Just a couple days ago."

"Oh lordy lord, man," Kelvin said. "So what cell are you in?"

"They got me stashed up in C-7." Both of the expressions on the faces of the other two men changed when LaMarcus gave them this answer.

"C-7?" Thomas asked. "Really?"

"Yeah," LaMarcus responded. He looked at his two friends and saw they had gotten a bit nervous. "What's going on in that cell, y'all?" In the south you're looked on as weird for saying *you guys*. "People act weird when I bring it up. When I got here the guards snickered after I was assigned to it."

Kelvin was quick to answer. "It ain't the room itself, LaMarcus. It's the guy who's rooming in it."

LaMarcus's face seemed to grow a confused look. "My cellmate? But he's just an old man. Honestly, I wonder how that guy ever got locked in here."

Thomas started speaking with a stern voice. "There's mixed stories going 'round about him. Some say that he ain't any harm at all. Those people say that when he talks it's usually ever about God or something like that. Religious kind of stuff. Most aren't sure what to think of him. He's not intimidating at all when you look at him, but most everybody doesn't want to go near him. Especially not since the incident."

LaMarcus was curious now. "What incident?" he questioned.

"That's the problem," Thomas continued. "Nobody around here wants to talk about it. It happened years before Kelvin and I showed up here. The inmates use the incident to prove that he's possessed by demons or some kind of thing. In either case, guards and inmates alike leave him alone because they're afraid that something similar will happen to them."

LaMarcus was starting to get concerned. "Well, what do you think?"

"One way or another, he's definitely different from everybody else in here, that's for sure. My advice would be to have as little conversation with him as possible, but always be nice to him when you do, just in case he tries anything," Kelvin answered.

"Right. And now I got a question for you, bro," Thomas interjected. "You hear anything from Drea before you got locked up?"

"No. I ain't heard from her for a long time. Not since you two were arrested," LaMarcus said.

"Oh. I was just wondering. I hadn't heard from her since that last letter she wrote to me," Thomas said.

"Yeah, she was really keeping her distance from everyone at home after you got hauled off. We tried to get ahold of her but she wouldn't pick up. I never did figure out why," LaMarcus said.

Thomas looked really grim. Kelvin decided to speak for him. "I bet I know why. She didn't want the gang around her baby."

LaMarcus was stunned. "Baby! I didn't know she had a baby. But why wouldn't she want us around it? We're her friends."

"Think about it, man. If you were a brand new mother, would you want a bunch of thugs around your child?"

"We're not thugs, Kelvin. We're family," LaMarcus retorted.

"Yeah, and look at where we are, LaMarcus!" Thomas snapped, not able to control himself anymore. "Half of our family is in jail. I found out that she was two months pregnant when I was arrested. By the time I get out of here, I'll have missed that baby's early years. And when I get out, I still don't know if she'll let me anywhere near my son."

"So what are you saying, Thomas?"

"I'm trying to find out how I got here, man. All that stuff we used to do when we were kids. All that stuff we did when we grew up in the gang. What was the point? What did any of it mean?"

"What are you talking about, man?" LaMarcus snapped back. "We did what we had to do to survive in our broken up lives. Our real families failed us so we were our own family. We did what he had to do to survive and get respect. And we even got our rep up in the process."

"Respect? Our rep? In that couple of blocks I might have some street rep, but in this city as a whole, whenever someone reads about me, they're gonna read about a man who missed the beginning of his child's life because he was in jail. The point is, now that I've seen this place, I don't want my son to end up here like I did. You and everybody else back home are still my family. I'd die for you guys...but I'm not gonna commit the crimes no more. I'm out of the gang."

"Same goes for me too, LaMarcus," Kelvin added.

"You got to be kidding me. After everything we worked for, you guys are going to just walk away?" LaMarcus said with a pressing tone.

Kelvin spoke back very calmly. "We want a future worth living for. We don't know what that is exactly, but a future hopping in and out of prison is not a future worth living for. We may be in our thirties by the time we get out of here"—they both had about five years on LaMarcus—"and what happens if we mess up again? We could be in our forties next time we see freedom. We had our fun, but now, maybe it's time to see that we're not kids anymore, and we need to make something of our lives while we still got one to live."

"I don't believe you guys right now." LaMarcus got up and walked away from them.

"Give it a couple years, LaMarcus!" Thomas shouted. "You'll understand."

LaMarcus raced back to his cell in unbelievable anger. He couldn't believe that his friends were abandoning the gang. As he dwelled on what he had just heard, he began to relive his life. All of the hurt and pain began to surge, which only angered him even more. He was so angry that he didn't even realize that his cellmate had entered the room.

It didn't take much for the old man to realize he was angry and in pain. Facing LaMarcus, he sat down on the edge of his own bed very quietly. A few minutes later LaMarcus began to calm down, and when he finally gathered his senses, he turned to see the old man on the other side of the cell with his hands to his head, which was bowed, and his eyes were closed. LaMarcus could swear that it looked like the old man was praying. LaMarcus couldn't stand the sight of it anymore.

"Hey!" he shouted. "Hey!"

The old man stopped what he was doing and looked up at him.

"What are you doing?"

"You looked like you were in some deep thought. I didn't want to disturb you, but wanting to help, I did the only thing I could do."

"Man, I didn't even hear you come in the room."

"Yeah, you were pretty riled up," the old man said. "So now that you've calmed down a bit, would you like to talk about it? Or would you rather keep it to yourself and have more episodes like what you just had?"

"Why don't you just shut up about it? Look, it ain't even any of your business," LaMarcus snapped at him.

"No, it's not, which is why I asked if you wanted to talk instead of demanding you to. I may not look like much, but if nothing else, I can listen."

LaMarcus still seemed unconvinced.

"Come on, LaMarcus. The only way you'll know for sure that you can't trust me is to trust me, and then I fail you."

LaMarcus rolled his eyes. "Or I could just not take the chance and stick with not trusting you at all."

"You're not willing to take a chance. You want to play it safe. Interesting choice, coming from someone like you; someone who's not been afraid to take a chance before."

"And how would you know that?"

"Son, if you had never been willing to take a chance, you never would have risked it all and ended up in here. It may have been for a stupid reason, but that doesn't mean that you're not willing to, pardon the expression, take a leap of faith."

LaMarcus chuckled a little at that response. If nothing else, this old man was crafty. "Very well, old man. Have it your way." So LaMarcus told him everything about what Kelvin and Thomas had just told him, at least as far as Thomas's baby and quitting the gang. The old man just listened to LaMarcus, never making a sound. When LaMarcus was finished, the old man pondered everything he had just been told.

"It sounds to me like your friends have really thought this through. Really want to do something more with their lives. What about you? Have you ever thought about your life meaning something more?"

"What are you talking about? This is my life. People know me and they respect me," LaMarcus said.

The old man snickered. "I don't think there is as much respect in living a criminal lifestyle as you might think. In either case, you want the right kind of respect. There's respect you get from earning it. You work hard at life and people will start to look up to you. Then there's respect you get from demanding it out of fear. Not all examples of this are bad, such as our parents or the police. There should be an amount of fear in our respect for these parties because they have been placed in power over us. But what then if you are not in that position, but you still demand respect through fear? That sounds a lot like terrorism to me."

Those last few words shook LaMarcus to the core. He never thought of it like that before. But the old man wasn't finished.

"It sounds to me, LaMarcus, that you're not really angry with them for leaving the gang and cleaning up their lives. You're really afraid that you'll lose your friends by their decision to go down one path, when you want to stay on the same one, the one that's comfortable to you. If I were to ask them, I'm sure they would say that they are scared too. Going down a path you're not familiar with is hard, but in their case, it's for a good cause. And I know that they want you to think about joining them too. If I were you, I'd do it. Don't be angry when I say this LaMarcus, but you're really not the prison type. You may never tell me why you got yourself locked in here, but deep down, I don't believe this is what you really want."

LaMarcus was a mix of emotions at this point, but at the top was amazement that this stranger could read him so well. Trying to act tough and deny it, he said in a low voice, "How do you figure all of that?"

The old man just smiled, looked at him, and said, "A friend of mine told me."

With that, he pulled up his covers, closed his eyes, and began to drift off to sleep. LaMarcus sat there completely confused.

What friend? LaMarcus thought to himself. Before he could question him any further, he could already hear the loud snores coming from the old man and realized the conversation was over. "Stupid, crazy, old fool," LaMarcus muttered to himself. Lying down, he turned to face the wall and fell asleep.

CHAPTER 3

A couple of months went by and a few more of these kinds of conversations came up. Whenever LaMarcus got the strength to ask Mr. Curtis how he came up with his answers, or how he learned certain things, the old man always responded with either, "my friend told me," or, "my friend taught me." While it irritated LaMarcus that the old man never gave him a straight answer, with each time he began to get as curious as he was irritated. Who exactly was this "friend" that he kept talking about? Was he still alive? Was it that this friend knew so much about LaMarcus himself, or was it things that were told to the old man that just so happened to fit with him also?

LaMarcus tried not to pay it too much mind, but the idea kept stirring in him all the same. He also kept thinking about all the rumors and the questions the other inmates had asked him. All too often he was asked how he was holding up or told by someone they were amazed he wasn't dead yet. LaMarcus also remembered the rumor Thomas had told him about the old man being possessed by demons. LaMarcus laughed inside whenever he heard that rumor. He would think, *if that guy is possessed by demons, they're some of the nicest demons I've ever met.* He still sensed something was different about the old man, but it wasn't a frightening kind of different. Besides, he was so used to the old man's antics by now that he hardly noticed or paid attention to him at all.

No matter how much he told people the truth though, they still wouldn't come anywhere near the old man because they remembered the incident. Even the new inmates tried to give LaMarcus a hard time based on what their cellmates had told them, which always ended with, "at least you're not the kid living with the guy in C-7." LaMarcus never bothered to ask the old man about the incident. As far as he was concerned, it was none of his business, and as much as LaMarcus was beginning to share with him, he figured that if and when the old man was ready to tell him, he would.

The only other thing that really got brought up in conversation was what the old man was listening to on the radio. He told LaMarcus that he used the radio to stay in touch with the news of the outside world. He only listened to two radio stations, one for his news and one for his music. The old man told him he rarely listened to the one with the music for the sole reason that the radio station had a bad habit of playing the same songs all day. As for his news station, he had very specific times in the day he would listen, and most of his listening actually occurred on Saturdays. He would keep the radio down low enough so he could hear it, but it wouldn't disturb LaMarcus too much, something LaMarcus appreciated because it made it easier to tune out what was being said.

Sometime later, a few months after LaMarcus had first arrived in the prison, he was out exercising on the court during rec time. He heard a deep growling voice behind him.

"Well, well, well. How fortunate for me that I find one of you punks locked away in here." (His language was actually a bit more extreme than that.)

LaMarcus turned around and saw a guy about his age who was as tall as he was but much larger than he was. The guy could've played a lineman in high school. LaMarcus looked him over and didn't recognize him, but once he saw the tattoo on his arm, he knew that he was from a rival gang, and that's all he needed to know.

"Hey, man, you know the warden's rules," LaMarcus piped up. "Let's not do this in here. I don't want any trouble anyways."

"No trouble, huh? I'd say this is not your lucky day," snarled the rival member. "No, I think this is the perfect place to do this. We're already in jail, baby. What more are they gonna do to us?" He started getting closer to LaMarcus as he said this. "You know that last time we had it out, one of your boys shot my brother."

LaMarcus started to get nervous, thinking this guy was out for blood. "Did he make it?"

"Yeah, he made it. He's all right," said the rival member.

LaMarcus breathed a sigh of relief when he said that.

"There's still one problem, though," the rival member continued.

"And what would that be?" LaMarcus asked.

"He has a scar." And with that, the rival member gave LaMarcus a huge shove backward. LaMarcus was so unprepared for it that his shoes got caught up and he took a hard hit to the ground. "For all that fear that my family went through thinking he wasn't going to make it, I'm gonna beat up on you just enough to make you think you're not going to make it."

The rival member had already bribed the guards not to interfere with what he was about to do, so they were nowhere in sight. How a prisoner bribes guards, only a certain few would know. Nonetheless, the rival, whose name was Big Tony, knew he had the guards in his back pocket.

Big Tony sized LaMarcus up like a lion about to pounce on a gazelle. LaMarcus had tried to get back up right away, but he busted his knee open pretty bad when he hit the asphalt. Putting pressure on it without the knee being dressed was out of the question. Big Tony, smiling and taking his time, walked closer like he was stalking LaMarcus. It scared LaMarcus enough that he thought this may be more than just a physical beating. LaMarcus was laying on his side, grasping his knee, but that only left a wide open target for Big Tony to kick, right in the stomach. Big Tony kept jeering at him, yelling at him to get up.

LaMarcus kept thinking about the days leading up to this. In all the time he'd been here and at the precinct before, nobody came near him. But now, here, it was at long last, and it had to be by a rival gang member. LaMarcus was more foolish though when it came to his pride. Not wanting people to think he didn't try, he found a fence to pull himself up with, the entire time being mocked and harassed by Big Tony. Once he finally made it to his feet, as predicted, he could barely stand. Big Tony got a sick look in his eye.

"Glad to see you still got some fight left in you. Unfortunately for you though, I'm gonna beat it out of you real fast," Big Tony snarled, pulling his fist back to give LaMarcus a Superman punch (kind of like Superman used to do to meteors in the old cartoons).

LaMarcus was starting to bend down a little because of his knee, so as Big Tony pulled his fist back, he lost sight of everything around him. As his fist began to come forward, something almost instantaneously blocked LaMarcus's face. Before Big Tony could stop himself, he clobbered the face of an elderly man who went flying into the fence. While Big Tony was trying to figure out what had happened, LaMarcus suddenly found some partially renewed strength and lunged forward, tackling Big Tony to the ground. (Not a bad feat for someone LaMarcus's size.) LaMarcus let out a fury of punches—any kind or amount of damage he could do. He didn't get too far along, though, when he felt a couple of hands grab him and pull him off.

"LaMarcus! That's enough! Stop it!" he heard a familiar voice say. LaMarcus took a good look and saw it was the old man speaking to him.

Big Tony began to get up for another attack when the old man whipped his head around and shouted, "Enough! Your business with this boy is over. If you have anything further left to take out on him, I suggest you do it to me."

"What are you doing? This ain't your fight, old man," LaMarcus shouted.

"Shut up, LaMarcus!"

LaMarcus was stunned. This was the first time the old man had ever snapped back at him like that before. Turning toward Big Tony, the old man continued, "Like I said, anything further you have to discuss, you take it up with me."

"Yeah? You gonna use your demon powers or something, old man?" Big Tony laughed.

"If I do, will you be so brave enough to find out?"

Big Tony just looked at him. He had heard the stories. He didn't know what the old man was really capable of, but he decided it wasn't worth the risk.

"You know what, I don't care. I think your boy's learned his lesson." With that, Big Tony walked off.

The old man turned to LaMarcus with a grim look on his face. "Come on," he said, "let's get you patched up."

"I could've taken him. I didn't need your help," LaMarcus said.

"That's not what it looked like to me. In any case, that's not the point. Where do you get the bright idea to start fights in here?"

"I didn't start that fight, old man. He came at me first."

"Well, you sure finished it, didn't you?" the old man said with a cold voice. "I bet you really feel like a man now, don't you?"

LaMarcus was surprised by the old man's tone. "Well, what was I supposed to do? Let him beat up on me?"

"It's not that you fought back, LaMarcus. It's not that you defended yourself. It's how you did it. You lowered yourself to his level. For one who cares about pride so much, where's the pride in that?" He paused for a moment then continued, "Come on, let's get you patched up."

As they started walking away, LaMarcus's curiosity got the best of him. "Hey, old man, how'd you know I was in trouble when none of the guards came?"

The old man just looked at him and smiled, saying, "A friend told me."

LaMarcus looked down, disgusted. "Of course he did."

The old man took him to a guard who ushered him to the prison's medical staff. After treating LaMarcus's wounds, a sergeant came in to question LaMarcus about what had happened. LaMarcus simply shrugged his shoulders and said, "I tripped out in the yard. I'm embarrassed to admit it, but that's what happened." The sergeant didn't really believe that was the full truth, but not wanting to mess any further with this incident, he decided to fudge the investigation.

By the time the two got back to their cell, LaMarcus's knee was really starting to writhe in pain. The old man did the best he could to help LaMarcus with his mobility. LaMarcus wasn't about to tell him, but with his knee in as much pain as it was, he appreciated the old man looking out for him.

"You're lucky that the knee is the only thing hurting right now," the old man said to LaMarcus.

"Yeah, I know. The thing that really surprises me is how long this actually took."

"What do you mean?" the old man asked curiously.

"The whole hazing, prison-fight thing. I thought for sure something like that would've happened the first week or so of me being here. Or even still down at the precinct. But now after so many months, I finally get something like this to come around."

The old man was intrigued and asked LaMarcus to expand on his story. LaMarcus told him about his whole experience at the precinct. The old man listened intently and hung on LaMarcus's every word.

"What do you think about all that?" LaMarcus asked after he had finished.

"I'm not sure," the old man replied. "I have my guesses but I'll have a better answer after I do a little research for you. For now, you just need to stay off that knee."

LaMarcus was more than happy to oblige to that. He made himself comfortable on his bed and began to fall asleep. He dreamed that he was in an orchard, looking for some apples or anything that looked good to eat. In the dream, he didn't seem to take into account that orchards aren't a common sight in the Mobile area, but nonetheless, LaMarcus walked, looking for something to eat because he was very hungry. Even though there were plenty of trees filled with apples and oranges and bushes covered with berries, every piece of food that LaMarcus tried to eat turned into ashes when he bit into it. He bit into an apple and jerked back at the taste, only to watch the apple turn into dust in his own hands. He didn't understand what was going on. No matter how much food he tried, nothing was real.

A voice began calling out to LaMarcus by name. The voice was a soft, soothing kind of voice, the kind of voice you would use to attract and lure a dog or some other kind of animal up to you. LaMarcus looked for the voice, but couldn't find it. With each call, the voice subtly began to become less gentle and slightly forceful, but LaMarcus still couldn't find the source of the voice.

Then LaMarcus saw a giant apple tree in the middle of this orchard, one grander than all the others he had seen before. This tree's fruit contained some of the juiciest, brightest, and largest apples he had ever seen in his life. Some of the apples looked to be about the size of some melons. His mouth watered at the sight, and he rushed to get a bite from one of the apples. He reached out his hand to grab an apple, and as he began to clench it in his hand, the apple, along with the rest of the tree and the orchard for that matter, disappeared. Suddenly LaMarcus found himself teetering over the edge of a high cliff. As he began falling down, he could see that he was heading for some sharp rocks on the edge of the cliff next to the ocean. He heard that same voice, only this time more sinister than before, call to him.

Still falling, LaMarcus turned himself toward the direction of the voice, and looking at the side of the cliff, he saw different moments from his life playing out in front of him as if it were a movie reel. It was clip after clip of horrible, horrible things LaMarcus had done or been a part of in his young life. The clips never seemed to end, and LaMarcus didn't feel himself getting any closer to the rocks. After what seemed like an eternity of falling, he finally looked back at the rocks to see them getting closer. He shut his eyes as he braced for his sure death, when he suddenly felt a strong wind change his course. Instead of plunging toward the rocks, he was now heading straight for the ocean.

As he neared the ocean, the waves began to circle almost like a monsoon. Then, within this monsoon, the waves actually pulled back, revealing something like a black hole in the middle of the ocean. The wind began to carry him straight through. LaMarcus was even more afraid now. With the rocks he knew he'd get death, but entering this freak incident of nature, he didn't know what to expect. Nonetheless, he had nowhere to go but straight through and braced himself just like before.

Though in the transition from the black hole to the stage it looked like he had only fallen a few feet, the pain he felt upon impact was as if he had fallen much farther. When he got up, he couldn't believe where he was. He was on a stage; not a theater stage, mind you, but a stage that could've been used for a rock band, only the stage he was on was clearly set up for something else. There was a podium set up on it for speaking, complete with a microphone. He looked out into the audience, and every seat was empty. The lights were on everywhere, including the stage, but then a spotlight shined on LaMarcus.

All of a sudden, a second voice called out to him. This one was clearly different from the first. This one was naturally gentle. It was not only gentle, but it was also powerful. It began to call to him by his name.

"LaMarcus."

The voice was so radically different from the first, that at the sound of it, LaMarcus couldn't even move. He froze like a deer in the headlights. He didn't know if he should answer, or if he should stay silent. Playing it safe, he didn't answer. Then the whole scene began to fade to black.

When the last speck of that room had finally turned to black, one last time, that second voice called out in its powerfully gentle voice, almost in a whisper.

"LaMarcus."

CHAPTER 4

LaMarcus shot up in his bed, trying to get a grip with everything he just saw. He was back in his cell, all right. It was the middle of the night, and there was the old man in the bed right next to him. LaMarcus was so freaked out by the dream he just had that he didn't sleep the rest of the night, but instead laid awake, trying to ponder its meaning, if it had one. He wondered if he should tell the old man about it. Maybe, if the time was right. But right now, he couldn't make any sense of what he had just seen. He had no confidence that he could do the dream justice by retelling it to the old man; all he could do was relay how disturbed he was by it.

In the next week or so that followed, the old man's demeanor seemed to change slightly. He was a lot quieter than usual, and hardly said two words to LaMarcus. LaMarcus wasn't complaining exactly, but it was definitely unusual to see him acting like this. In fact, it was so unusual that LaMarcus didn't really know what to think, and the whole thing was really starting to make him uncomfortable. To LaMarcus, it looked like the old man was in a deep state of thought. LaMarcus thought about what Big Tony had said in that confrontation about the old man having demon powers. Could the old man be meditating and trying to conjure up something? Whatever he was doing apparently required a lot of concentration, and LaMarcus was just trying to enjoy the peace and quiet while it lasted.

Two weeks had gone by since LaMarcus had that dream, and still the old man barely ate, drank, or spoke. For the first time since he had arrived, LaMarcus actually felt worried and concerned for his cellmate, and he couldn't stand the silence any longer. He waited until one night when everything seemed to be a little quieter after the lights out call from the guards. When it seemed like everything was all clear, he finally broke the silence.

"Hey, old man," he piped up. "You doing okay over there?"

The old man looked up at him, and it almost seemed like life was beginning to return to him. "Oh, yeah, I'm doing okay," he replied. "I've just been thinking about some things for a while."

"What kind of things have you been thinking about that's been keeping you from eating and talking?"

"Oh, lots of stuff can do that for me. The world's a very grim place when you look at it in a broad sense." He looked around the cell a little bit more, and when he noticed that LaMarcus wasn't trying to shrug off the conversation, he continued. "You ever loved someone before, LaMarcus?"

It was a rather random question in LaMarcus's mind, even random for the old man to ask. For once though, it wasn't a question that LaMarcus minded answering.

"Oh, I've had a lot of girlfriends over the years. Some of them I've been real interested in, and others I dated just to say I dated them. Didn't really mean anything special. I don't have one right now. Might have to look for one when I get out. Heard some girls get turned on by a man who's been in prison." He started laughing. "Am I right?"

The old man just stared at him with a disgusted look on his face. On the one hand, he was happy to see LaMarcus actually loosening up around him. On the other hand, it was pretty obvious what the only use was that LaMarcus had for girls.

"That's not the question I asked," he said rather sternly. "I said, *have you ever loved someone before?*"

LaMarcus thought for a minute.

"Well, no. I mean, I've thought a lot of the girls I've gone with looked good. Real good. But I was never interested enough to actually *love* them, love them." He paused for a little bit and asked in return, "Have you ever loved someone before?"

The old man took a deep breath and answered, "Well, sort of. I mean, I loved her, but I never got the chance to fall in love with her. You know what I mean?"

"I think so. Kind of like back in the hood. All of us boys have grown up together and we're like family. We would die for each other, and in that sort of way, we all love each other. We just don't ever say that we do."

"Right, that's close enough," the old man said. "She meant a lot to me, but I never got the chance to have the deep kind of love for her that I knew in my heart I had."

"Well, why not?" LaMarcus asked.

"Well, believe it or not, I wasn't always the bold, talkative person that I am today. Back then I was very timid. I often formed ideas in my head without any solid proof for those ideas being there. I actually went to school with her. Always looked forward to the classes we had together. But I kept my distance because I always made the decision for her that she wanted nothing to do with me in any regard. My interest grew and grew and I began to talk to her a little more, but always like an idiot and never enough to really establish a good friend base with her."

"So you never told her how you felt?" LaMarcus asked.

"Well, I did tell her through a letter. And even though I never heard anything back, I would still cling onto the hope that maybe… someday…it could happen." He took a deep breath as he continued. "Then one summer, it came to my attention that her father had passed away. I realized I had to put my feelings on hold in order to be there for her. Even though I hadn't talked to her for a while at that point, I made sure that I would not make the mistakes I had made before. And with a friend's help, I was able to say the right things that needed to be said. It wasn't until much later that I realized that my desire for her was one that would never be granted."

LaMarcus had a confused look on his face. "How did you figure that?"

"It was made clear to me that I could be a friend for her when she needed it, but as for anything else, it just simply wasn't meant to be, or at the very least, it simply wasn't meant to be yet." He let out a small laugh. "As long as I have breath, I will still hold on to the hope for a chance, even if it is hopeless and only a fool's hope. There are times I would rather be a foolish person with hope than a wise person with emptiness. But those times are for very certain things.

"I will say this though, even though I never ended up with her, I would never take back the chance I had to be the friend she needed during one of the darkest hours of her life. I know it helped her. Her own mom even told me so. Some days I wish I could've done more, and other days I know I did exactly everything I was supposed to do. None of it was for nothing. And in turn, she helped me. She was the first one. I had never boldly stood to help and encourage those who came in my path before her. If I hadn't done what I did with her, I may not have ever started that path of helping people. I am a good listener, if nothing else, and I've been through a lot and seen a lot. And with a lot of help, without which I would never have succeeded in life, I've done the best that my limited human body and mind can do to try and point people in the right direction."

LaMarcus was bewildered by that last comment. He said he'd walked a path of helping people, and yet here he is in jail. Must've messed up somewhere down the road.

After he had finished reminiscing about the past, the old man paused and took another deep breath, as if he knew what he was about to endure next was challenging. "So, why don't you tell me about your brother?"

The old man had a real knack for changing conversation on the fly. LaMarcus seemed to hesitate when he started speaking.

"Oh, my little brother, Jacoby. Far as I know, he's doing okay. I got to see him before I was arrested. He's about thirteen now. He's a real good athlete. If he plays football he could be like a wide receiver or a running back. Something like that. He's a lot quieter of a kid, real different from me. I think about him sometimes. All that's left in the house right now is him and Mama 'til I get out. But I think they'll do alright. Jacoby's still too young to be allowed in any gang activities, so for now, the only thing he needs to be worrying about is school. To be honest though, I don't think he'd do it. Jacoby never seemed to take interest when I'd tell him about the things we do. He even asked me why we did those things once. I tried to explain to him, but he didn't buy it.

He said, 'sounds pretty stupid to me.' Maybe school will work out for him. He's a lot brighter and better in school than the rest of us were."

As LaMarcus spoke, the old man hung on his every word. He certainly was a good listener like he said.

"That's really good to hear, LaMarcus," the old man said. "I hope it works out for him. But I wasn't asking about him." LaMarcus looked up with a shocked and confused face. The old man continued, "I was asking you to tell me about your older brother."

LaMarcus stared at him in disbelief. How could this man know he had an older brother? How was it possible? LaMarcus never told him about his older brother. He had mentioned his kid brother, Jacoby, before, but not his older one. LaMarcus felt a swirl of anger and confusion rise in him, but even though he didn't want to talk about it, he found himself opening his mouth and speaking.

"What's to tell about him? He was two years older than me. He was a legend on the streets. Everybody loved him. I even gained my status because I was 'KayShawn's little brother.' I've enjoyed my life on the streets, don't get me wrong, but KayShawn was born for it. He lived for the thrill, the edge, roaming the streets like it was his kingdom. He was destined to take the leadership spot someday. I looked up to him. He was like a hero to me. I remember when I officially joined the gang, he was so proud of me. I was fourteen at the time, and he was sixteen. Fourteen is the minimum age of people allowed in the gang. KayShawn taught me everything I know, at least all he could teach me."

LaMarcus's voice began to get higher and his eyes began to water. "Sometime after I joined, I can't tell you how long after, we got in a firefight with a rival gang. It was actually the night that Big Tony was talking about when he was fighting me the other day. I don't even know what it was about. All I remember is Kay standing next to me. We were fighting back together, and then I heard a shot fire. I turned to look at him as he started falling to the ground. He had got clipped right in the chest. He looked up at me but couldn't speak. I had dropped down to try to carry him away, but before I could move him, he died in my arms. I screamed his name over and over, but nothing I could do could bring him back. The guys from the other gang realized what had happened, and they took off running. And I was left to explain to my family what had happened."

The old man looked at LaMarcus, somberly. "I'm sorry, LaMarcus. I know it must've been hard for you and your family."

"Mama didn't speak a word to anyone for a whole week. Jacoby often stared at KayShawn's stuff or pictures of him. Me, I relived that moment every night for at least a year."

The old man buried his head in his hands as LaMarcus recounted everything to him. It wasn't an act or anything, and LaMarcus could see it. The old man genuinely cared about everything that was being said to him. But nothing could've prepared LaMarcus for what was about to come out of the old man's mouth. He looked at LaMarcus and very solemnly stated, "I'm sure it must've been difficult for your father as well."

LaMarcus began to feel more anger rise, not necessarily at the old man, but at the mere mention of his father. "My father? Yeah, it hurt him. I mean, KayShawn was his first born, his pride and joy. Whenever he was home in-between prison visits, it was always KayShawn who he wanted to be around. KayShawn was just like him as far as living for the gang was concerned. But KayShawn still had a protective instinct that my father had abandoned long ago. Whenever my father came home from prison visits, he was either drunk or he would bring home the booze so he could get drunk. And whenever he was drunk, he'd start beating on me and Jacoby and even Mama. He started doing it when we were both real young and KayShawn was in juvie.

"One day, though, he made the mistake of doing it when KayShawn was home. KayShawn jumped him after he started beating us and he knocked my father out cold. My father never came around the house again after that, claiming it was because he had disowned KayShawn. But after KayShawn died, he was back and at his worst. He blamed me and Jacoby for KayShawn's death, and he attacked both of us. When I tried to fight back and protect my little brother, he stopped attacking Jacoby and put all his attention on me. The worst part was that he enjoyed it. Mama always said he never wanted more kids after KayShawn and this was proof. He beat me within an inch of my life. He did it because he knew I didn't have the strength to fight back, and because KayShawn wasn't around to protect me. That was the last time I ever saw him. For all I know, he's dead or back in prison."

LaMarcus's story was very disheartening for the old man, to say the least. The news is riddled with stories of fathers who hate and disown their children; it's well known that there are fathers out there who abuse their children. These problems exist. No one is oblivious to it. But to hear it from the mouths of the victimized children themselves is a very humbling experience, no matter how many times you hear it. The old man wasn't finished, though. He became somber and he began to speak with a very low voice. "That's not all he did, is it?"

LaMarcus looked up with that same bewildered face he would get when the old man was able to read into him. "What?" he responded, trying to deny what he was being confronted with.

"You said yourself that he beat you within an inch of your life. He didn't want to just beat you. He wanted to dominate you. He wanted to show you that you would never be better than him. He wanted to show you that he was strong and that you would always be weak. So it wasn't enough to just beat you up."

At this point, LaMarcus made no effort to hide his anger. All of the hurt and emotion from that night began to surge through him and he was on the verge of exploding. The old man didn't let up.

"All those times in and out of prison. He took more away from there than what he was supposed to, didn't he? He took what he learned in prison and brought it home to you."

LaMarcus began to clench his fists, doing everything he could to suppress his anger.

"It was no wonder you were hurt," the old man said as he got up and stood close to the bars of the cell. "He was your father. He was supposed to love you. He was supposed to be there for you. He was supposed to protect you. But he didn't protect you. He stole from you. He...BETRAYED...YOU!"

LaMarcus stood up sharply, standing on the opposite side of the cell with his back toward the wall and the radio, facing the old man and the cell bars.

Tears formed in the old man's eyes as he declared, "He took your innocence away."

The moment he said it, LaMarcus felt a dagger pierce through his heart. Tears gushed from his eyes; anger and rage seemed to flow through his body like a rushing river. LaMarcus began to speak again; his voice was half filled with sorrow, the other with burning rage. Through tears and gritted teeth, LaMarcus exclaimed, "Who…told…you? How…did you…know…about that?" He could barely get the words out.

The old man just stood there, as if he was about to embrace Armageddon. He very quietly said, "My friend told me."

That was the final straw for LaMarcus. His sorrow-filled eyes turned to eyes of evil and vengeance. LaMarcus immediately screamed and sprinted toward him (or as much as he could in that small cell), and he straight up tackled the old man like he did Big Tony weeks before. Rage and anger controlled LaMarcus's every move as he crouched over top of the old man, punching him repeatedly in the face with swift, crisp strikes. Then, with every single hit, he started speaking.

"I…am so…sick…of hearing…about…your…stupid…friend!" After saying "friend" he gave an extra hard right hook. Then he got up, and the old man rolled on his left side. LaMarcus then proceeded to give him four hard kicks to the stomach. For the fifth and final one, he reached back and kicked the old man with all the energy he could muster and as hard as he could. By this time, the guards had finally realized there was commotion and rushed to the cell to see what was happening. When they got there, they found the old man lying on the ground with a bloodied face, struggling to breathe, and LaMarcus, who had moved back to his side of the room and was standing by his bed.

"What happened here?" yelled one of the guards. Looking at the old man on the ground, he yelled at LaMarcus, "Did you do this?" LaMarcus said nothing as he breathed heavily, still trying to ventilate the anger within himself.

One of the other officers figured that it didn't take a rocket scientist to know what had happened, so he spoke up. "All right, let's go. Come on."

"No! Officers, it's okay." The old man was writhing in pain on the ground, trying to speak. "Please, just leave him here this time. I know what the warden's rules are. I know that you're supposed to take this kid away, but I'm asking you, please, to overlook everything this one time. I said some things that made him angry. He acted out of emotion, not just for the sake of starting a fight. Please, I'm begging you. Don't punish this kid."

LaMarcus turned his angry face toward the old man. On the inside, he was floored in amazement. This guy was unbelievable. Here he had just gotten the crap beaten out of him, and he was still defending LaMarcus in front of the guards. Who in the heck is this guy?

The guards didn't want to defy the warden's rules, but the old man clearly wasn't seeking to press charges. Since he was so adamant about it, they decided to leave LaMarcus be.

After they left, LaMarcus laid down in his bed while the old man struggled to get back into his. They both fell asleep facing their respective walls, as silence hung like a shadow over the cell.

CHAPTER 5

LaMarcus's world began to spiral down into its darkest place at this point. Everything the old man had said drove him to his limits every single day. Having to relive the events of his brother's death and his father's actions afterwards was as if he had been cursed to never be free of those images. The fact of the matter was that LaMarcus had kept those events suppressed in his heart for years, but now that the old man had confronted him with it, the images would not leave his mind. His past was the source of further paranoia around the prison as he would get stares from the other inmates and the guards. No doubt about it, he was being haunted. Every time he remembered his brother dying in his arms, and every time he remembered the evil look on his father's face, droves of thoughts of a demonic nature entered his mind so as to take an already tragic scene and disproportion it even further.

It wasn't just during the day that LaMarcus was being haunted. LaMarcus would wake every night in a cold sweat and would sometimes scream in his sleep. The same nightmare would play over and over again every time his head touched a pillow or he closed his eyes. It was the same dream that he had several nights before. The only difference was that when he was falling down the cliffs to the ocean before, he'd look back at the cliff to see the images of his wrongs. Now when he turned, included with those images were the images of his brother and his father. The first voice was becoming more angry and persistent. The second voice was also becoming more persistent, but it stayed just as gentle yet powerful as before.

The more he thought about these dreams, the more LaMarcus started to feel insanity creeping in. He tried not to sleep, but he had seen the nightmare enough that even when he was successful in depriving himself of sleep, it played in his mind even when he was awake.

One night LaMarcus awoke from the nightmare and found the night air of the prison to be much cooler than it normally was. He looked over at the old man who was fast asleep with the deepest sense of peace about him. It angered LaMarcus to see him so peaceful while he was disturbed and restless. LaMarcus began to wonder if the old man really hadn't put a curse on him. However, it wasn't an unusual thing to see him at such peace. There wasn't a time that LaMarcus could think of where the old man wasn't at some form of peace. The thing about it was that the old man never did any of that meditation stuff or tried to conjure anything up. Everything seemed to flow very naturally from him as if he didn't have to work for or be the source of his peace. It was all a very strange scene for LaMarcus.

And yet, for whatever reason, seeing the old man lying there with such peace like that caused LaMarcus to settle down and reflect back on the time since he first came to this prison. If he was ever going to figure out the old man's secret, then maybe the previous encounters would give him some clues. Plus, he had insomnia anyway, and he was in prison, so what better way to spend his time?

So much about the old man was a mystery. For all of the crap that LaMarcus had given him since his arrival, he was still one of the nicest, gentlest, most peaceful and mysterious individuals he had ever met in his young life. He remembered the way the guards had snickered about his rooming with the old man when he first arrived. He remembered the vibe he felt when he first met him; how even though the old man was another inmate, LaMarcus just seemed to know he wasn't any danger or threat to him. That vibe never disappeared. In fact, as he looked over at the old man again, he had a sixth sense that no matter what LaMarcus said or did to him, the old man wasn't going to fight back....at least as far as anything physical. When it came to mental or emotional things, this guy was a masterful tactician. He was as precise as a surgeon when it came to picking apart LaMarcus's mind. LaMarcus had heard of people who were able to read others like a book, but this old man read him a little too well—as if he had been there side by side with him during his whole life.

LaMarcus's head swirled with confusion as he tried to wrap his head around how the old man knew so much about him when he had never told him anything. How did he know he had an older brother? As angry as it made LaMarcus that he brought it up, how did he know what his father had done to him? I mean, it's no secret that that kind of stuff happens in prisons across the country, but how did he know that his father did that in the aftermath of KayShawn's death? What made him think that LaMarcus wasn't the prison type, or even the criminal type for that matter? How did he know that he was scared of losing his friendship with Thomas and Kelvin? How did he know he was in a fight with Big Tony?

Even in some of the other conversations they had—like when the old man reassured LaMarcus that his mother didn't hate him for going to jail, but really was afraid for him—did he know about KayShawn back then? Or was that reassurance based off the brief mention of his father during that conversation? No matter what kind of conversation they had, every answer the old man gave him was always backed up with bold confidence. It was the kind of confidence that could even make proud men shake. But it wasn't just any type of arrogant confidence. The old man did have confidence in what he was saying, but for him, the confidence seemed to be less in what he was saying and more in where he was getting his words from: this "friend" person he would always talk about.

This particular time, when LaMarcus thought about the old man's friend, instead of confusion or unyielding rage as a reaction, he was a lot quieter and curious about him. In fact, the more LaMarcus thought about it, the more aware he became of the mystery of this "friend" rather than the old man himself. This friend always seemed to hide in the shadows of their conversations. This friend the old man would reference every time they had a conversation, whose every word he seemed to draw on.

Thoughts LaMarcus had had before about the friend began to resurface. Never mind how the old man knew so much about LaMarcus. If he was getting his information from this friend, then how did the friend know so much about him? Was this friend at the prison? He must've been if that's how the old man knew about the fight LaMarcus was having with Big Tony. That, then, left the biggest question of all. Who exactly is this friend of his? What's his name? Any time the old man ever mentioned him, it was always as a friend or "my friend." LaMarcus had often disregarded this person as an imaginary friend or as the voices in the old man's head, but supposing that this was indeed a real friend, then just who was he?

Something else was really starting to bother LaMarcus as well. It was the same thoughts he had the night he attacked the old man, but now that he was calm, they came back and really started to sink in. Not only was this guy able to read him like a book, not only did he know the deep, dark things about LaMarcus's past, but after getting beat down by a young kid who at that point practically hated him, the old man begged and pleaded for the guards to let him stay there. How did he know LaMarcus wasn't going to beat him even more? Why would anyone put their life in potential danger like that? But more importantly, why would he even want him there at all after what had happened? That was the part that LaMarcus didn't get at all. If it had been the old man who had attacked him, LaMarcus would've wanted him sent to the other side of the country (after getting in a few good shots first).

LaMarcus wrestled with these thoughts, but he simply could not come up with a logical answer. It couldn't have been that LaMarcus had hit him too hard. The old man was too sound in his voice when making his plea. No matter how hard he tried, nothing made sense. It was the most irrational thing a human being could do in that situation, and yet he did it, and LaMarcus could not make heads or tails as to why.

LaMarcus's night was not over, though. As soon as he fell asleep, the same recurring nightmare began as before. This time, though, a new element was added to it. After landing on the stage and looking out into the audience, LaMarcus saw something that wasn't there before, or at least he hadn't noticed it before. There was a television screen on the front of the balcony wall. On the screen was a message in big bold letters. It said, **Greater love has no one than this: to lay down his life for his friends**. Underneath that was another sentence that said, **I have called you my friends**.

As everything faded to black, the second voice appeared on cue, only this time it had more to say: "LaMarcus, I AM." LaMarcus woke up abruptly and pondered the new elements in the dream. The two messages had been about and included friends. He thought about the first sentence, and then he thought about the way the old man had stepped in for him on more than one occasion. The old man had tried to be his friend ever since he first arrived. There was no denying that. Then he thought about the second sentence. Was the old man trying to say that he considered LaMarcus his friend? Why would he after the way LaMarcus had treated him? The old man had no reason to call him his friend, much less show love for him as a friend. And then there was the voice. It clearly wasn't the old man's voice. So what was the purpose of this voice, saying, "I am"? I am what?

LaMarcus thought about the timing of this new part of the dream. It came about now, at the same time as these two sentences on the screen, but why? Maybe they were related. "I am friend, I am a friend." LaMarcus tried to fit the pieces together, when suddenly, a light just clicked in his head. *Friend. I am. I am the friend.* He had nothing to base this off of, but it just seemed right to assume that the second voice in the dream was revealing itself to be the voice of the old man's friend. The more he thought about it, the more logical it seemed. LaMarcus almost broke into tears at the thought that this revelation might be true.

As he began to think about this "friend" concept more, it only began to bring new questions into his mind. Once again, if the voice and the friend are one and the same, then what is the name of the friend? For that matter, who is the identity of the first voice? What about the rest of the dream? He looked over at the old man again, who was still as sound as ever. The more LaMarcus tried to piece everything together, the more he realized that this was something far beyond any of his understanding. He thought that even though the old man was still only human, he had demonstrated an uncanny ability to pull things out from midair. Maybe he could do the same thing with this dream. But would he talk to LaMarcus again after he had beaten him up so badly the other night?

The only thing that LaMarcus could do was hope that the old man would look past that night and help him. The fact that he had stood up for him that night was, if nothing else, a glimmer of hope that he may be willing to look past it. LaMarcus had a gut feeling, though, that talking to the old man about the dream and that night was going to have to happen if he was going to get any answers.

Realizing that it was already late in the night, LaMarcus thought it best to wait until the next night so they would have plenty of time to discuss everything. All throughout the next day, his heart and his mind raced with anticipation. He wondered what the old man might be able to reveal to him, if anything.

When it finally came time for LaMarcus to say something to the old man, he wasn't sure that he could do it. He laid on his back, staring at the ceiling, thinking about everything that had happened one last time and trying to find the courage to talk to the old man again. As he was going over everything in his head, he didn't realize it, but he was starting to think out loud. It was like he was whispering to himself. The old man could hear it, but he didn't respond to it.

Finally, LaMarcus couldn't take it anymore. Still lying on his back, he spoke up and asked, "Why'd you do it?"

The old man stirred a little, rolled over, and looked at LaMarcus. "What're you talking about, kid?"

LaMarcus answered with a little harshness in his tone. "The other night. I beat you down. I hurt you. I left you lying on the ground. You could hardly breathe. Yet when the guards came to take me away, *you* stood up for *me*. Here I am, somebody who just attacked you. I could've attacked you again. I'm practically your enemy…and yet you defend me. Why? Who does that? Who puts themselves in potential danger to protect an enemy?"

The old man looked at him very somberly. "LaMarcus, I've met a lot of people in my life who turned out to be enemies—very great enemies. You…are not my enemy. Although even if you were my enemy, I'd still do the same thing, even if to no avail. It's just in my nature."

LaMarcus shook his head. "That just doesn't make any sense at all."

"I suppose it doesn't make any sense from a common point of view. But the way I look at things is a little different. They call themselves my enemies because what I stand for poses a threat to them and how they live their lives. All I do is hold them accountable to how they live their lives and try to get them to wake up to reality. I do this because I don't want those people to be my enemies anymore. I approach them with a genuine concern, trying to show love, and letting them know their lives mean something to me. They don't see it, however. They want what they want, and so they push me back."

The old man paused a moment and then continued. "But you, you're something different. Sure, there have been times where you have pushed me back, but your mind is much more open to the things I say to you. In more ways than you even can think of right now, your mind is ripe for harvesting. I think it's because your whole life, you've been searching for something real. And I think that you're wondering right now if I have or can lead you to that real thing you've been searching for."

"I wouldn't even know what that real thing is," LaMarcus said.

"It doesn't matter," the old man replied. "The question is that if it really is real, are you willing to diligently, actively start seeking it, whatever it is? This place would be a good place to start looking. There are no distractions here. There's no escaping here. You're left with two choices: waste your time, or spend your time wisely. It's the same out there, but out there it's harder. Out there, you have distractions. Out there, you can escape. You can avoid the problem. But when you really start to think about what it is that you are searching for, it is in our best interest to also ask, *why am I searching for it?* Obviously you're missing something, else you wouldn't be searching for whatever it is. You're incomplete without finding this real thing. You're inadequate by yourself because you don't have the thing that you've been searching for. And eventually, what it all boils down to is that when you ask the why, all the channels lead back to you, and you realize that in some form or another, you are the problem."

LaMarcus looked up at him as he said that.

"You are the problem," the old man continued. "So that 'it' that you're looking for, that 'real thing'…is the solution. When a person is sent to prison and they get fed up with how they've been living, that's the question that they ask themselves: *how can I turn my life around?* Most of them try and fail. Some are able to succeed, but it's only because they found the right solution—not the right solution for them, but the right solution. Everyone else, though, that doesn't get fed up, they don't get fed up because they don't feel the need to make a change. They don't feel they're doing anything wrong."

The old man got up and sat next to LaMarcus on his bed. "I can tell that something has been eating away at your heart. You've been thinking about what I said, about you not being the prison type."

"Yeah, I have," LaMarcus said.

"That's why I defended you the other day. I knew the warden's policy. I didn't want to see you sent to another cell with God knows who as your cellmate, where you could've been in real danger. Plus, I have a sixth sense about these inner struggles that people have, and I wanted to be there for you to help you with yours. Lord knows that no one else in this old shack would care."

"That's just it, though," LaMarcus piped up. "Why would you care, especially after I've treated you the way I have?"

"Because, LaMarcus, I can see untapped potential inside of you. You have depths within you that you don't even know you have. I've talked to my friend about it the other day, and he agrees with me. In fact, he showed me more about you than even I had thought to be true. I know you don't like me talking about him, but it's true. I'd say that most everything, if not everything, I know about you was told to me by him."

LaMarcus knew it. Somehow he knew the old man wasn't getting everything from nothing. He had a source. Even still, how did the source know so much about his personal life? The whole ordeal with his father was never reported to the police, mostly because of the boy's criminal record and his mother was afraid of what his father might do if he found out it was reported. Instead of getting angry, LaMarcus found himself speaking the things he was thinking.

"This friend of yours must be really something. To know all that personal stuff about me, to give you all the advice you've given me, which I'm sure includes everything you just talked about."

The old man nodded. "Oh, yes. He's really special."

LaMarcus gave something like a half-nod back and said, "I might have to meet this guy someday."

The old man smiled as he laid back down in his bed. "I sure hope you do, LaMarcus. I sure hope you do."

CHAPTER 6

Over the next couple of days, LaMarcus spent some time thinking about what was said to him—about making some changes in his life. Deep down, it was something he wanted to do, but he still needed to convince himself. He still wasn't sure what the old man was proposing. It sounded to him as if the old man knew what this right solution was but was waiting to see what LaMarcus's decision would be. As much as deep down LaMarcus wanted to do better, he didn't know where to start. He began to think that maybe he couldn't start. Could anyone fix someone or something like him? True, he was softer than a lot of the other inmates, but that didn't mean LaMarcus hadn't done his own share of terrible things in his life. Even if the old man or even his friend offered their help, the idea set before him felt overwhelming if not impossible.

No sooner did LaMarcus get discouraged about the whole thing, when something seemed to tug at him to just do it. After all, what did LaMarcus really have to lose? He was already in prison. He was already deemed a failure and worthless and dangerous. If he tried to do better and messed up, nobody would even think twice about it.

All of these thoughts rolled through LaMarcus's head, but in the end, he found he was nudging himself to do it. The old man had never steered him wrong before, and if he was willing to help him, then LaMarcus thought this could work out after all.

Even though he had explained why he did what he did, LaMarcus still didn't understand why the old man was paying him any attention at all. Ultimately, LaMarcus thought that maybe understanding that would come along with this whole life changing thing the old man had in store for him. Perhaps he had to adopt these new things before he could begin to understand the old man's actions.

Having made up his mind, he came back to the cell after rec time was over to give the old man the update. The old man walked into the cell, and LaMarcus spoke up almost immediately.

"Hey, listen. I've been thinking about what you said. I know that just about everything about you is strange and real different to me. But I also know that even though I don't get it, I want to get it. I want to be able to understand that. I see the kind of person you are, and I know that I want to be that kind of person too. So I guess what I'm saying is that any help you'd be willing to give me, I'd be very grateful."

The old man looked at him. "And have you given any more thought about my friend?"

"This friend…you really trust him that much? You lean on him that much?" LaMarcus asked.

"LaMarcus, I can honestly say that I wouldn't be who I am today without his help. I owe everything to him." The old man spoke with such reverence that it made LaMarcus even more intimidated. This friend really must be something.

"Well, if that's the case, then I want to meet him."

The old man's head popped up, and he looked intently at LaMarcus. "What did you say?"

"If he means that much to you, and everything you're saying is true, then I want to meet him. If he helped you that much, then maybe he'll help me too."

The old man started to grin after LaMarcus said this. LaMarcus could see that he wanted to burst with excitement.

The old man finally nodded and said, "That's good, LaMarcus. That's really, very good. I'm so happy to hear you say that. I don't think you'll regret it either when you meet him."

LaMarcus began to push the conversation forward. "Well, I guess we got to figure out how we're going to meet on the outside so you can take me to him when we get out of here."

The old man chuckled a little. "Oh, LaMarcus. We don't have to do anything that elaborate. Because, you see, my friend is already here."

LaMarcus sat up further at those words. He had wondered if this friend had been in the prison, and now the old man was confirming. "He's here. At the prison? Who is he? Another inmate? A guard?"

"Yes, he is here at the prison, but more specifically, he is here right now."

LaMarcus got the most puzzled look on his face. He looked around, and there was no one there but himself and the old man. "Um, can you see him right now?"

"No, I can't see him. But I know he's here."

LaMarcus was starting to get worried now. He was putting his trust in the old man who, up until now, had never steered him wrong. Now suddenly he was having illusions or thinking of imaginary friends. Or maybe this was the whole demon power thing the other inmates talked about all the time.

The old man could see the worry in LaMarcus's face, so he continued. "LaMarcus, do you remember the disagreement we had about the radio when you first got here?"

"Yeah," LaMarcus answered.

"Do you remember what I said about it?"

LaMarcus just looked at him blankly. "You said you didn't want anybody to touch it."

"Yes, I said that, but I also said something else about it."

"Dude, it's been a while since then. I can't remember everything we said that day."

"Try harder, LaMarcus," the old man continued. "I said something about its value."

LaMarcus thought hard about it. "You said it was your second-most valued possession." The old man nodded, and LaMarcus thought about it some more. "Come to think of it, you never did tell me what your most valued possession was."

"Let's be honest, would you have really cared at the time?" the old man asked with a slightly grim voice.

LaMarcus lowered his head a little and said, "No, I guess I wouldn't have. So what is it anyway?"

"My most prized possession is the only other thing I've ever asked for during my time here." As he said this, the old man walked to the end of his bed, near his pillow, and lifted up the mattress. He reached under the mattress and pulled out a small, yet thick book. He put the mattress down, put both hands on the book, and walked towards LaMarcus with the title of the book facing toward LaMarcus.

LaMarcus squinted to read the title, until he could finally make out the words, *HOLY BIBLE*, on the front cover. LaMarcus froze, not knowing what to do. This was the exact opposite of him having demon powers.

The old man spoke once again. "This is my most prized possession."

LaMarcus struggled to get his words out. "So you're actually some kind of religious freak, then?"

"Nope," the old man replied. "I can't stand religious people or religion. They're pompous and prideful and in love with their own knowledge. But if you're asking me if I'm a Christian, then yes, I am."

LaMarcus was so confused by this statement. But instead of dropping the conversation, he forced himself to hear the old man out. "I don't get it," he said. "You call yourself a Christian, you're holding a Bible in your hands, and you say you're not religious?"

"Right. It's really, very simple. Christianity is not a religion. It's a relationship with God Almighty. Religion and religious people will only scratch the surface of the intimacy that God desires with His people. A true Christian will grow in a relationship with the Lord that is so deep, they can call themselves a bondservant and even a child of the Living God."

LaMarcus, for whatever reason, was not making the connection, so he asked the old man, "So what does this have to do with your friend who we can't see?"

"It has everything to do with my friend. You see, my friend, the one who I trust with my life, the one who I lean on His every word, the one who made me the man I am today, and the one who told me everything I have learned and spoke to you...is Jesus Christ."

LaMarcus was floored. If that were true, then that would explain how the old man knew everything that he did. But LaMarcus had spent his whole life believing that God and Jesus didn't exist, or at the very least, if they did exist, they didn't care about him. But if Jesus was the friend that expressed obvious interest and concern for LaMarcus, then his whole life he had been wrong. Part of him, though, still had doubts.

"Anything I've heard about Jesus has been about a guy who lived like two thousand years ago. How could He still be alive? And if He was, what would cause Jesus to care about someone like me?"

"LaMarcus, you're going to have to accept the fact that there are some things that you're not going to be able to understand right now. What I am proposing to you is this: if you want to understand those things and get your questions answered, I'd like to spend time with you every day reading from this book. It may be frustrating at first, but if you'll be patient and do this with me, I promise you that God will reveal the answers to your questions. I'm not forcing you to make the decision here and now to follow Christ. All I'm asking is that you hear and listen to what God has to say to you, and then you choose what you want to do."

LaMarcus was amazed at how little pressure was being put on him. Once again, he thought to himself that he had never been steered wrong before by the old man. "All right, I'll give this whole thing a shot."

The old man smiled as he started to put the book away.

"Um, Mr. Curtis?"

The old man looked back at him, astonished that LaMarcus hadn't called him "old man."

"Do you think maybe we could go ahead and start now?"

"Absolutely," Mr. Curtis said. "And the best place to begin is at the beginning." With that, Mr. Curtis opened up his Bible, and they began to look at Genesis. Mr. Curtis read to him all about the creation of the world and everything in it. LaMarcus was fascinated. He had heard the arguments that God had created the world before, but never once in those arguments had he ever heard how God had created the world. It was far different than anything he had expected. If he were a god creating a world, he would've put on a fantastic light show of sorts, displaying all of his great power. But the real God was different. At first it seemed anticlimactic that He would create the world with something as simple as speaking, but then it dawned on him. God didn't have to do anything fancy to create the world. He was so powerful that He created the world and everything in it just by speaking it. Mr. Curtis described it like this: God desired it to be, and so it was. He willed it to be, and it was. He spoke it into existence. He created the world and breathed life into it by creating light and plants and animals and eventually humans.

They read about the creation of man and woman, how Adam was made from the dust of the ground and Eve was made from the rib taken out of Adam. "I've heard a comedian say once that this rib must be the one that had given men the ability to read minds. So now that the rib was gone, we can't read our wives' minds even though they want us too," Mr. Curtis joked.

"I bet there were some interesting conversations in the Garden, then." LaMarcus added.

"Not really. As of this point, the world is still perfect as God intended it to be. At this point, Adam and Eve don't have fights with one another. She respects him as the man, and he loves her as the woman."

"A world without fighting. Sounds like paradise to me," LaMarcus said.

Mr. Curtis nodded. "Exactly. It was. The Garden of Eden was literally a physical representation of heaven on earth. Adam did not have to work the land; the land grew everything itself. No animals were carnivorous. There were no harsh winters to prepare for. There were no storms or natural disasters that could appear and destroy their lives. These things didn't exist. Adam and Eve had only the one task of caring for the Garden that God created for them. Aside from that, all they had was all that they needed. They had each other, and more importantly, they had a personal relationship with God Almighty, Himself. Every day, Adam and Eve would walk in the Garden with God. They would laugh. They would talk and talk about good things because there were no life problems for Adam or Eve to deal with. There was nothing for them to cry about or get angry with. These things didn't exist yet."

LaMarcus was intrigued. "So, how did they come about?"

"Let's keep reading. We read that the two of them had only one rule from God that they had to obey, correct?"

"Yeah, they could eat from all of the other trees but not the tree of the knowledge of good and evil," LaMarcus answered.

"Correct. Now, let's look at what happens in chapter three." Mr. Curtis read to him about how the serpent, who was controlled by and representing Satan, convinced Eve to eat of the tree of knowledge and also used her to get Adam to eat of the tree as well. He read how when the Lord came to them again, they ran and hid because, after eating the fruit, they realized they were naked. God, having found them guilty of disobeying him, put his just punishments on the both of them and was forced to evict them from the Garden.

After finishing the chapter, Mr. Curtis looked at him and said, "Now, what do you think about that?"

"It seems a little harsh. I mean, they messed up, but there's no reason to just cut off the relationship like that."

Mr. Curtis shook his head. "No. God didn't cut off His relationship from them. He simply removed them from the Garden."

"Yeah, but Mr. Curtis, I've done bad things my whole life, and my mama never kicked me out of the house."

"Yes," Mr. Curtis refuted, "But your mama is not God. While it's true that God is a Father to those who believe in Him, He is also more than just a mere parent. He is God: righteous, just, and holy. He could not be God if His standard of justice was not carried out."

"But I don't get it. Yeah, okay, they ate from the tree one time. They made one mistake. I thought God was supposed to be forgiving and merciful. He kicked them out of their home for one screw-up. It doesn't seem very just to me."

Mr. Curtis looked at him very sternly. "It was God's forgiveness and mercy that stayed His hand from slaying them on the spot for disobeying him in the first place."

LaMarcus was taken aback at this response. He had never considered that side of it.

"LaMarcus, do you know what sin is?" Mr. Curtis asked.

"Yeah, we just never call it sin at home. I've heard it called 'wrong choices,' 'wrong actions,' that sort of thing."

"And based on that definition, would you say that what Adam and Eve did in the Garden was a sin?"

LaMarcus nodded back. "Yeah. They were told not to do something, and they did it anyway."

"Right, but here's the thing. Sin is much more than just wrong choices or actions. What about wrong emotions?"

LaMarcus contemplated, but didn't answer.

"You want to know what the Bible says about sin? Anything done without faith is a sin. Anything that is not of God is sin. By its very definition, sin is separation from God. It's not possible for this to happen, but let's pretend a person could live his entire life with correct morals, making no wrong choices, and living a 'good' life without God. He still would have committed sin because God was not included in his life. Sin is all of this, and it first came into the world the second that Adam and Eve ate of that fruit. Before, all they knew was how to do right. Now they had knowledge of both good and evil, which meant they now knew how to commit evil things.

"Sin entered the world like a veil covering the earth. Its impact, its influence affected the earth. The earth became violent and natural disasters were formed. Certain animals became carnivorous. The ground would grow thorns and thistles. All of this was a result of the influence of sin. It entered the world and it entered Adam and Eve. Because they chose to disobey God, the purity in man's heart was replaced with a sin nature; a nature as in something natural. All it took was one time for sin to become a natural thing in the design of man. It was not God's original design. It was foreign to God's design. Before, man did not know how to sin, but now that he had, what was to stop him from sinning again? It was now natural to him. It was his nature. And because we all come from Adam and Eve, we are all born into sin. We are all born with a sin nature, and we share in the punishment that the first couple received."

LaMarcus shot back. "That's not fair. We weren't the ones who went against Him in the Garden."

"No," Mr. Curtis responded, "But think of all of the things you have done that went against him. Romans 3:23 says that 'ALL have sinned and fallen short of the glory of God.' The Bible also says that 'there is none righteous, no not one.' And as such, we share in the punishment. Women received increased pain in childbearing and a desire to usurp the authority of the man in the house and society at large. Men received a curse to the ground that they would have to work the land to grow food and provide for their families. And because the man, as the head of the two, failed the woman, he brought death into the world. Remember what God had said about eating the fruit, 'thou shalt surely die.' Satan tricked

Eve into thinking that they would not die, as in if they ate it, they would die immediately. However, what he did not tell her was that they would die eventually because, where before death did not exist, now that sin existed, and death is a by-product of sin, they would at some point in their lives pass away from the earth. As the Lord said, 'for dust thou art, and unto dust shalt thou return.'

"But when the Lord said they would die if they ate the fruit, He was not talking of just a mere physical death. He was also referring to a spiritual death. Remember, LaMarcus, that everything God does in the physical realm is to be viewed as a picture of what He does in the spiritual realm. Where once before here on Earth, Adam and Eve walked with God, now they were physically separated from him. But they were also separated from Him spiritually. Their bodies did not die immediately when they ate the fruit, but their spirits did. They endured a literal spiritual death because the purity of their hearts was replaced by sin. And this, above all else, affected their relationship with God.

"You said earlier that it didn't seem fair to kick them out of the Garden for one sin. The Bible says very clearly that God hates sin. God is just. He cannot allow sin to go unpunished. In Romans it says that 'the wages of sin is death.' In other words, for one sin that gets committed, the just punishment is death. How much more, then, for a lifetime of sins? Even more so, God is also holy. Sin cannot come and enter His presence. That is why God had to evict them from the Garden; they had become tainted with sin.

"So let's sum this up: After we die, which itself is a by-product of sin, we must be punished by God for the sins we have committed. One sin deserves one death, so a lifetime of sins deserves a lifetime of death, or rather, an eternity of death. This must take place somewhere that is separate from God, which is where we then get hell from. Sin, death, and hell are all related, and they are the path and destiny of the human race, because we have turned from our Creator."

LaMarcus felt a rush of depression and horror fall on him. "So if we are all destined for hell, then we are all doomed. What hope do we have?"

Mr. Curtis, who had been getting excited before, settled down and said, "This is where we see the mercy and grace of God come to play.

We deserve death for our betrayal of the Almighty, but even still, God has made a way for us to be forgiven."

LaMarcus, with angst in his voice, asked, "How?"

Mr. Curtis answered, "In due time, we'll cover this in greater detail, believe me. But even at the point of history with Adam and Eve, God made a promise to Adam, Eve, and the serpent, who was Satan. Speaking to Satan through the serpent, God said in chapter three, verse fifteen, 'I will put enmity between thee and the woman and between thy seed and her seed; he shall bruise thy head and thou shalt bruise his heel.'"

LaMarcus looked puzzled. "What exactly does that mean, Mr. Curtis?"

"Basically, what God is telling Satan is that one day He would send someone to the world. Satan would be at constant war with this person. The bruising of his heel means that Satan would deliver a painful blow to this person, but it would not be fatal. The person, however, would bruise Satan's head, which would be a fatal blow. This person, as we'll see throughout our Scripture study, will go on to be called the Savior of the world, the promised Messiah, the coming King, and many other names. He is the hope that we can have. He is the lifeline of grace and the bridge back to God the Father."

LaMarcus sat up as if a light bulb went off in his head. "Jesus. It's Jesus, isn't it? The one who would deliver the fatal blow to Satan?"

Mr. Curtis nodded his head.

"But how? How could Jesus alone be what we need to get back on God's good side?"

"It's simple really, but I think that for today we should take a break. It's a lot to take in."

"Yeah, it is," LaMarcus said.

CHAPTER 7

The next day, after the morning meal, Mr. Curtis sat down on his bed while LaMarcus trudged somberly back to his. "Are you ready to start again, LaMarcus?"

"Yeah," he said quietly. "Let's keep going."

Mr. Curtis took a deep breath before he started. "You know, LaMarcus, I feel like I have to share this with you. Usually I'm very blunt and straight to the point, but with you I've felt the Lord say to share with you a different way, and that is simply reading the Bible together. I also, though, don't want to seem like I'm avoiding answering any questions you have. So if you would like me to skip straight to the New Testament, I can do that, and then we can go back to the other books in the Old Testament."

"No, it's okay. Hearing all of this stuff is pretty heavy, but I'll be okay with it."

"All right," Mr. Curtis said. "What I want to do is read a little more history. It is important to understand the significance of Jesus to the world, but it's also important to understand the significance of Jesus to the nation of Israel. After we read some more history, I will go ahead then and skip to the New Testament for the sole purpose of driving the meaning behind all of this home. Is that okay with you?"

LaMarcus nodded.

"If after that you decide you want to continue, we can go back and observe the books that we skipped over." From there, Mr. Curtis opened up the Bible to where they left off in Genesis. LaMarcus learned about the lives of many faithful believers as well as corrupt men of evil. He learned the lineage of the world from Cain and Abel to Noah to Nimrod and to the family of Abraham.

Mr. Curtis asked LaMarcus, "Do you know why the world hates the nation of Israel today?"

LaMarcus shook his head.

"The truth is that underneath all of the petty, made-up reasons, the reason they hate Israel is because the prince of the world, Satan, hates Israel. Israel is the seed that God is making mention of here to Abraham. The Jewish people are a part of the family of Abraham. God is revealing that the promised seed of the woman in Genesis 3, Jesus Christ, would come to the world through the lineage of Abraham—very specifically through Abraham's son Isaac and not Ishmael. And between Isaac's sons we see the lineage narrowed down even further through Isaac's son Jacob. This is why, as we will see later, the Lord introduces Himself as the God of Abraham, Isaac, and Jacob. It is very important to understand this lineage. As such, Satan has always been at war with the Jewish people, for they would be the ones to bring the Messiah into the world."

Mr. Curtis then went on to talk about Jacob's twelve sons. He explained that this time all of Jacob's sons would be included in forming the nation of Israel. The twelve tribes of Israel are the descendants of Jacob's twelve sons. LaMarcus took a real interest in the story of Joseph and hearing about his dreams he received and also about his time spent in prison. Obviously it reminded him of his similar situation, along with the mysterious dream that he had. Mr. Curtis pointed out at the end of Genesis, right before Jacob passed away, he told his sons that the line of Judah would receive the kingship for the future nation of Israel and also the coming King Messiah.

The next couple of days they began to look at Exodus and all that the children of Israel went through while in Egypt. LaMarcus learned of the great Hebrew leader Moses who God used to lead the people out of Egypt into the Promised Land God had spoken of to Abraham. They spent quite a bit of time on the Law God had given the Israelites in the desert as they moved from Exodus to Leviticus, Numbers, and

Deuteronomy. LaMarcus learned what became of the Israelites after Joshua took over as the leader and they endured the battle at Jericho.

After this, they skipped ahead and looked at 1 and 2 Samuel and 1 and 2 Kings. It was here that LaMarcus learned of the first king of Israel, King Saul, and how he fell from God's favor by doing things his own way. It was then that God would raise up another who would be, as far as Israel's early history, Israel's greatest king, King David. It was during King David's rule that Israel was at the height of its greatness. LaMarcus also learned that the Messiah who would rule Israel from Jerusalem would be a descendant of King David. It is when the Messiah rules Israel that she will be a great kingdom for the first time since King David; only the Messiah will make it better and more glorious than ever before.

They also touched on the great prophet of God, Elijah. "You will hear Elijah's name mentioned when we talk about Jesus, so it is best to know now who he is," Mr. Curtis said. Elijah, of course, was the prophet who prayed and held back the rain for a time and had challenged the prophets of Baal on Mount Carmel.

Another day, then, was spent discussing the downfall of Israel. Briefly looking at 1 and 2 Chronicles, Mr. Curtis showed him the growing evil in the heart of Israel, starting from the time that King Solomon, David's son, had turned away from the Lord. The kingdom went back and forth between serving God and serving themselves, usually more the latter, until the nation split into the kingdom of Israel and the kingdom of Judah. Both, however, would eventually come under the rule of the wicked Babylonian king, Nebuchadnezzar. It was here that Mr. Curtis skipped forward to Daniel, showing LaMarcus how Daniel would gain favor with Nebuchadnezzar and eventually the Persian kings when the Medo-Persian Empire overthrew the Babylonian Empire. Mr. Curtis promised that one day they would go back and look at the other chapters in Daniel, but right now they were still looking at the history.

A little more than a week had passed since they first began their studies. Mr. Curtis looked at LaMarcus and said, "There is still so much I would love to share with you in the Old Testament; things in Isaiah, Jeremiah, Joel, Amos, and, well, everything. But I think for now, we will go ahead and look at the first four books of the New Testament: Mathew, Mark, Luke, and John. Are you finally ready to learn about Jesus?"

LaMarcus was more than ready. He was ready at last to see how Jesus would fulfill the promise to bruise Satan's head. He was ready to learn how Jesus would restore Israel to its former glory. He was ready to learn how one man could be the Savior of the world for all time. Mr. Curtis would hop around between the four Gospels, trying to paint the whole picture for LaMarcus. He shared Christ's virgin birth and how the Magi, the three wise men, came to pay homage to the future King of the Jews. He shared the various miracles that Jesus performed among the people. He instructed LaMarcus to pay careful attention to Jesus's words, for it was in His teachings and not the miracles themselves where the value lied.

The more LaMarcus read a teaching from Jesus or read about another miracle He did, the more he wanted to hear more about Him. Many of these things he had heard before, but he had never read them from the Bible itself. Now that he was, and considering all of the history they had looked at, he began to see everything from a different perspective. Jesus's name gets tossed around all of the time, but LaMarcus realized that this was a great mistake, because if you look at Jesus from the perspective that the Bible is true, you'll realize that Jesus was the most selfless, wise, amazing person to ever live. And no wonder all of this was true of him. The Apostle Peter came to understand by God that Jesus Christ was in fact not only the promised Messiah, but also the Son of God. LaMarcus admired the way Jesus answered the questions and objections of the Pharisees. After all, being the Son of God, who better to know how to answer their questions? LaMarcus started to think about his own life. Who better to know the answers to his questions than Jesus?

After reading all about the ministry of Jesus, LaMarcus found the tone of the accounts changing. Jesus went to Jerusalem for the celebration of the Passover feast and was met by people with palm branches, shouting, "Hosanna!" The Pharisees, however, had grown a deep hatred for Jesus. They believed He was speaking blasphemies and sought to kill him. LaMarcus didn't understand this at all. Here, Jesus was doing all of these great things, and if they were supposed to be the religious leaders who had studied all the prophecies of the Messiah, how did they not see Him for who He was?

Then the unthinkable happened. Jesus was betrayed by one of His own disciples, Judas Iscariot, for thirty pieces of silver. He was delivered into the hands of the very people who hated Him. They began to strike Him, spit on Him, mock Him, and later after His trial, He was whipped and flogged and mangled to where He was hardly recognizable. LaMarcus couldn't believe what he was reading. For one, these were Jesus's own people doing this to Him, but also, He never made a sound of resentment to them. LaMarcus began to understand now why Mr. Curtis had done the things he did a while back. He had learned it from Jesus.

After this, LaMarcus read about the trial with Pontius Pilate and the long road that Jesus took to be crucified at Calvary. Barely able to stand, He was forced to carry a heavy cross that healthy men would have had difficulty carrying. Mr. Curtis explained to LaMarcus about Roman crucifixion. It was an execution that was designed to not only kill a prisoner, but more specifically to humiliate him. And the more LaMarcus read about it, the more he could see that this was, aside from physically and emotionally painful, very humiliating. It didn't seem to make sense that God Almighty (who LaMarcus came to realize by reading John that not only was Jesus the Son of God, but also God Himself) would reduce Himself to human form and suffer such humiliation like that.

Finally, he read where Jesus was nailed by His hands and feet to the very cross He had carried, and the Romans lifted the cross up to display Him to the crowds who only continued to mock him.

"It all had to be done this way to fulfill the prophecies of the Scriptures," Mr. Curtis said. "We read later on in the New Testament that when Christ was dying, He carried the sins of the world. In other words, picture all of the sins committed throughout time, from every white lie to every bloody genocide, all latching on to Jesus on the cross like leeches. That's why God the Father couldn't even look on His Son anymore. He put all sin upon Himself, though He was still sinless, so that by the shedding of His blood, we may at last be free from the hold of sin. You see, when a person accepts Jesus Christ into their life, they are spiritually washed in His blood, which acts as a covering. When God the Father looks at us who have given our lives to Christ, He no longer sees a wretched sinner, but rather a new creation who is washed in the blood of His Son, because only His Son is Holy enough to come before the Father. That's why Jesus told His disciples before He died that 'no one comes to the Father except by Me.'"

"But, Mr. Curtis, even if that is the case, what good would it do to follow Jesus when even he, the Son of God, died? Doesn't that show a God that can still be defeated?"

"It would if that were the end of the story. You best keep reading, because there's more," Mr. Curtis said.

LaMarcus kept on reading as he was instructed. As he read the next few chapters, his eyes became wider and wider. For you see, LaMarcus was reading the chapters that revealed Jesus was, in fact, not dead. After three days, some of the women who had travelled with Him went to the tomb where He was buried to find His body no longer there. An angel met them, telling them that Jesus was risen from the dead and that they should inform the disciples. Jesus would later meet the women on the way back, and He met the disciples twice in the Upper Room and lingered on the earth for several days before He ascended to heaven.

"Now, you see," said Mr. Curtis, "Not only did Jesus pay the price for our sins, but He also took back the key of death and Hades. That means that no longer does Satan have complete control over us. We now have a choice. We can choose to follow Jesus. We are no longer bound to an eternity of separation from God Almighty."

LaMarcus swallowed those words hard. Jesus was capable of all of that? He truly was One who had no equal. It was unbelievable to think about.

Mr. Curtis could somehow sense that LaMarcus wasn't taking this as personally as he needed to. "Do you not see how this relates to you personally, LaMarcus? You asked, when we looked at sin entering the world, 'what hope do we have?' Jesus is that hope, and this is how. Through His death and resurrection, Jesus has paved a way to salvation; for all who find it, yes, but also for the ones who don't find it. The offer is still there to them, but they have to make a choice whether to give their lives to Christ as He did for them or to keep their lives and reject what Christ did. You also, now that you know the truth, must make that choice. You see, He died for you too, and He loves you so much that if He had to do it all over again just for you, He would."

Mr. Curtis continued. "Christ is offering you right now the only true hope, the only true freedom that you will ever find in this lifetime. All you have to do is choose to repent from the way you've lived, and give the rest of your life to follow Jesus. Even though salvation is available to all, only those who accept it and want it will receive it. Often times they want it but will not give up their desires, their sin nature, and without repentance, which is what giving up sin is, they will never be able to receive the salvation of Christ. Christ came to save everyone, because the Lord desires that everyone be saved. It wasn't just the Jews who put Jesus on the cross that day. We all have sinned. So we all at some point have put Jesus on the cross."

LaMarcus was cut down to the core when Mr. Curtis said those words. It was true. He knew it was true, and the thought was unbearable to him. He would have never thought it was so personal before, but to hear that he, by his sins, had contributed to the death of Jesus, who was God in flesh, he fell to the floor and started crying.

"God, I'm so sorry," he cried out. "Please forgive me for putting you on that cross. Forgive me of all these things I've done, things that go against you. I don't deserve what you did for me, Jesus, but if you can do all of that, then I know you have the power to change who I am. I can't do it myself—if I could, I wouldn't be in this hole right now. I guess that's why you had to bring me here, so that I could see. Well, Lord, you've got my attention. If you did all of this for me who didn't deserve it, how can I not do the same for you who does deserve it? I will follow you Lord, from this day forward, if you'll take a weak, scrawny kid like me. Thank you, Jesus. Thank you."

Mr. Curtis was welling in tears. "The Holy Spirit helped you say that prayer, LaMarcus. I believe now that Jesus has heard your prayer, and He has sent the Holy Spirit to you to breathe life into you and your spirit. The road ahead of you is not the easiest, but it is more than worth it, because even after the resurrection, the story is still not over. One day, Jesus is coming back as King to reign over the earth, and He will execute the greatest display of justice and vindication for His people Israel, both Jew and Gentile, and will cleanse the earth of all unrighteousness. Our bodies will be resurrected and transformed into a new body, which He will give us, and we will live forever with him. It will be the time and place when heaven and earth will meet. Oh, what a glorious day that will be. I am so proud of you, LaMarcus. Here at long last you've answered the call that Jesus has been making to you. God has given me such joy to witness the birth of a new brother in Christ."

"He has been calling for a while, hasn't He?" LaMarcus said, choking back tears.

"Yes, He has. He's been calling you for a long time. And it's been intensifying the past year or so. I believe that's why He sent you here, like you said, and sent you to the same cell as me. He's been so desperate to reach you, He's even been calling you in your dreams."

LaMarcus looked up when he said this. "What do you mean, He's been calling me in my dreams?"

Mr. Curtis looked at him curiously. "Have you forgotten the dream you've had the entire time you've been here?"

LaMarcus stopped and thought about it. In all of the Bible studying, it had been a while since he had given that dream any thought. Assuming his theory that the second voice was indeed Mr. Curtis's friend who he now knew to be Jesus, then yes, indeed, Jesus had been calling to him this whole time.

"You're right," LaMarcus said. "But how did you know about the dream? I haven't had a chance to tell you."

"The same way I knew about the rest of your life as if I had been there. The Lord showed me everything through a series of dreams. When He showed me your life, that was several weeks ago, and as a result, that was when I barely ate, drank, or spoke. I felt such sorrow for you after seeing what had happened, I just couldn't do anything. Sometime later, when you were having a rough time sleeping, I asked God to show me the dream you were having that was making you so violent in your sleep. God honored my request, and not only did He show me the dream, but I can also tell you its meaning. It will make a lot of sense to you now that you have accepted Jesus."

"Yes, please, tell me. I've got to know what this dream means or else I may go insane."

"It's really, very simple. Think about the orchard you were walking in and the fruit you ate that turned to ash in your mouth, for example. The orchard was your own little world, your own little paradise that you would walk around in with a set of blinders to reality. That's why the fruit would turn to ash. The fruit represented your desires that you tried to obtain but truthfully didn't count for anything. The large tree with the large apples is a picture of the tree of knowledge. When you grabbed at it and the orchard disappeared, it was a symbol of realizing the orchard and the tree to be a trap and a fake. The first voice you heard was Satan's, trying to lure you into the trap. As you fell down the cliff toward the sharp rocks, and you looked back at all your sins, this symbolized a classic tool of Satan's: using your past to get you to keep failing. But the wind that carried you away from the rocks and certain death was Jesus. Going into the portal in the ocean was a representation of coming to Christ, similar to how baptism is an outward demonstration of the change God has made internally.

"As for the stage you land on," Mr. Curtis continued, "well, your hard landing means you'll go through some rough times to get there, but that stage is your future, should you allow God to guide you there. Who knows what you may say on that stage, but the reason young folks get sent to old ones like me is so the old ones can teach them the things to say when they get there. We have the experience, but you young people have the fire, so it's important that we get you trained. That's why the audience was empty. You haven't learned everything you're going to say yet. But as you do, I would bet those seats start filling up real fast."

CHAPTER 8

The next day, LaMarcus was still overwhelmed at the revelation he had received and the change that had just occurred within him. He knew in his heart, and he believed that Christ had saved him. And now, LaMarcus was ready to begin the rest of his life as a follower of Jesus. He didn't know what else the Bible would have to teach him, but he was very hungry for the Word that it would provide.

Also hungry for breakfast, LaMarcus was on his way to the morning meal, and he ran into his old buddies from the hood, Kelvin and Thomas. When they spotted him, they could tell he was extremely happy, overjoyed even, about something. It was odd. They had seen LaMarcus really happy and excited about things before, but this…this was somehow different. LaMarcus didn't have his typical ego-fueled swag about him. There was a swag in his step, but it was just different from anything they had seen from him before.

"Hey, man, where've you been?" asked Kelvin. "We ain't seen you in forever."

LaMarcus smiled. "I've been doing a lot of thinking and studying here recently."

"Studying?" interjected Thomas. "What've you been studying that's kept you from finding us at rec time? And why is it anytime we see you in here, you're always with that old man? What's going on, bruh?"

"Remember back when y'all were talking to me about leaving the gang and making a change in my life?" LaMarcus asked his friends. They both nodded at him. "That's kind of what I've been doing. I've been making some decisions for my life, and the results have been beyond words."

"Really?" asked Kelvin. "What did you decide on, if I might ask?"

"Y'all aren't going to believe this, but I decided to give my life to Jesus Christ." Kelvin and Thomas stared at him, eyes wide and mouths dropped.

"I'm sorry. You decided to do what?" Kelvin repeated.

"I've decided to follow Jesus. I'm a Christian now." LaMarcus answered. The two of them just looked at him in disbelief. If you had asked them five years ago if they thought LaMarcus would ever do something like this, they would've told you there was a better chance for all of the guys from their hood to play hockey, something you could get beat up for in their part of town.

"Okay, what did that old man do to you?" asked Thomas. "Where did he hide the real LaMarcus?"

"He didn't do anything, Thomas," LaMarcus answered. "This was my decision. I am the real LaMarcus. I've got the same body but a new nature, because the old one just wasn't cutting it anymore."

"Man, you sure he don't got you under his demon powers or something?" Kelvin asked.

"No, he doesn't have me under any kind of demon powers. He doesn't have them. What I found out, y'all was that if I wanted to really change my life, I couldn't do it myself, because I'm human. I'm bound to mess up. But Jesus, He's the only one who could fix me up and make me more than I ever thought I could be. And He can do the same thing for the two of you too, if you let him."

Kelvin and Thomas were stunned to hear this kind of talk coming from LaMarcus. Hearing all of this, Thomas had had enough.

"LaMarcus, we asked you to think about doing better, not devote yourself to some fanatical, hate-based religion," Thomas said.

"Now, wait just a minute," LaMarcus said, offended by what Thomas had just said. "Christianity is not hate-based. It's based more on love than anything else in this life could ever hope to be. God loved us so much that He sent His Son, Jesus, to die on a cross to redeem us in the eyes of the Father for all those who believe in him. He rose again, after being dead for three days, to free us from the power of Satan, and He's coming back again to reign as King and bring justice to all the unrighteous."

"Give me a break, LaMarcus," Thomas said loudly. "Do you have any idea how ridiculous you sound right now? That has got to be the most unrealistic, stupidest thing I have ever heard in my life. You're hanging the rest of your life on an imaginary fairy tale and not even a good one, either. This is real life, LaMarcus! We don't have any type of gods that can just whisk our problems away."

"No, God won't take our trials away from us, but He will be there to help us through them. And as for the sin problem, it's a battle. It's a war that has to be waged, but Christ gives us the strength and ability to fight it so that the more we, through Christ, drive sin away, the more we can replace that sin with Christ. And as a new Christian, I know that those battles are still ahead for me, but even now, I know that Jesus has already put a change in me. I'm not the same person I used to be. I don't have to be anymore. And as I continue to walk with Him, I'm going to do everything I can to imitate Jesus, because I know that He won't ever leave me."

"How, LaMarcus?" This time it was Kelvin who spoke up. "How do you know that he won't leave you or that he even exists?"

"It's actually quite simple. It's because He lives inside of me, and I know I can trust in Him because He is a Living God." It was a powerful answer. LaMarcus didn't understand how he was coming up with these answers, but he knew in his heart that they were the truth. "And by the way, Thomas, Christianity isn't a religion. It's a relationship with Jesus Christ, and I hope that someday you'll seriously consider accepting Jesus's offer for one."

Thomas and Kelvin didn't say anything more after that. They both just shook their heads and walked off.

When LaMarcus met up with Mr. Curtis again back at the cell, he told him the whole story. He expressed his great disappointment that his friends didn't listen to him about Jesus. Mr. Curtis did his best to encourage him.

"Don't get down, LaMarcus. Until the moment comes that they die, they will always have a chance to accept Jesus. The best thing that you can do for the two of them is pray that the Holy Spirit one day convicts them, just as He convicted you. And speaking of which, the wisdom you displayed without having learned any of it yet, that was clearly the Holy Spirit speaking through you. In time, LaMarcus, you will begin to fully understand the truth to the words you spoke."

LaMarcus nodded his head, and Mr. Curtis went over to his bed to straighten out the sheets. LaMarcus couldn't get one thing out of his mind. Once again, the idea of Mr. Curtis having demon powers came up in a conversation. Obviously, this wasn't the case, but why did so many people think he did?

LaMarcus looked up and asked in a low voice, "Mr. Curtis, we've known each other for a while and have come a long way since we first met. But in all the time we've known each other, I've heard about this thing that happened here called the 'incident.' I've heard it mentioned from other people, but I've never heard details, and I've never heard you talk about it. So I guess I'm asking if you could please tell me about it."

Mr. Curtis's old shaggy eyes grew very remorseful as he thought to himself about that day. He looked at LaMarcus and said, "Of course, I will. I believe I do owe you that much, that you should hear about it from me. It's not a day I like to remember that often."

Mr. Curtis continued: "The guards in this prison didn't always use to avoid me like the plague. In fact, it was just the opposite. They use to beat me on very frequent occasions. For such suffering is actually a part of the Christian walk. We all will face hard times, but such suffering as great physical beatings, persecution, and even death, these are the kinds of sufferings that will inevitably face each person who calls themselves a servant of God. Jesus taught that 'no servant is greater than his master.' All of the followers of the world hated Jesus. How much more, then, will they hate the ones who follow him?

"Jesus suffered greatly on His journey to the cross. Jesus once said, 'You will suffer for My name's sake.' We are all called to experience suffering just as our Master did. It comes in its various forms, but it is vital and a requirement, nonetheless. There is joy to be had in suffering. It is in the midst of our sufferings that we can grow the closest to Jesus. And out of it, we can become as refined as pure gold. And some are even called to martyrdom. Dying for the faith is the greatest honor any Christian could receive. It's not anything that's pleasurable to us, to be sure. But it's not about what's pleasing to us; it's about what's pleasing to Him. If He wants us to give Him honor and glory through suffering, then I say it is both an honor and privilege to be doing and be in the will of God."

After taking a minute to catch his breath, Mr. Curtis continued. "Not long after I first got permission to have my Bible, the guards heard I had it. They didn't like me having it at all, so four of them decided to do something about it. They all came down to my cell to give me an extra special beating. That day, I just happened to have my Bible out and was reading it, when they came to the cell door. I stood up to greet them and brace for my upcoming beating. This time, though, since I had it, I grabbed hold of my Bible and held it tightly. The first guard in the room seemed very offended by this. I watched as his eyes grew wide and the grimmest expression of evil came upon his face. He came at me and reached out to grab my Bible. His desire was to rip it away from me and more than likely destroy it before my eyes, so I didn't let him have it. We struggled for possession of the book, and when I wouldn't give, he reached his hand back to punch me in the face. As his hand started to go forward, it suddenly stopped. He just stood there, white as snow, as if he had just had a heart attack. His eyes turned to a colorless white. I had seen before when people die. I had seen before, people taking their last breath. But their eyes were always closed. His eyes were open, and even though it happened in an instant, it seemed like a slow motion video as I saw the life leave his eyes, and for that matter, the rest of his body.

"Thinking I had done something to his buddy, the second guard rushed me and lunged for my Bible. This time, however, no sooner did he get his fingers clasped around the cover of the Bible, the same thing happened to him, and he dropped to the floor next to his fellow guard. The third guard, though startled by what he had seen, felt it was up to him to avenge his colleagues. He then decided to come at me himself, but he only managed a few steps before he, too, fell to the floor with no life inside of him. The fourth guard by this point was pale white. He looked down at his friends and then back up to me. Instead of attacking me, he did the smart thing and ran the opposite way to inform the captain and the warden. I'll give him this, though, he told them exactly what happened. He didn't lie or do anything to get charges brought upon me.

I think it was because he was too frightened. Unfortunately for him, he had had his own share of beating fun at my expense before, and I found out a couple of days later that after he told everything, he became very sick, went home, and passed away at his house. Since then, no guard or inmate has dared to come near me."

Mr. Curtis continued. "As I've said before, the Lord will not necessarily spare us from suffering, but this time was obviously different. When it came to this Bible, God was saying enough is enough. I truly believe God protected me that day. Who knows what they may have done? But don't ever say that God is not faithful. He protected both me and this copy of His Word that day, because He did not want anything to happen to me until I met you. The Lord had His plan in mind, and He wanted me here so you could not only have a cellmate who you could trust, but also one who could introduce you to Himself."

LaMarcus looked at Mr. Curtis. "I think the Lord was protecting me too," he said. "I wondered for the longest time why no one tried to haze me when I was at the precinct. Some guy thought I had an angel looking out for me. Maybe I did. Maybe they wanted to attack me but didn't do it because something was holding them back."

"I would say that it is a very strong possibility," Mr. Curtis responded. "We can say with absolute certainty, though, that He was indeed protecting you. God had a plan to get you here to reveal Himself to you, and I was the one lucky enough to be picked by Him to pass on to you all that I've learned. And He still has a plan for you yet that neither one of us knows right now. In time, the Lord will reveal it, but until then, all we can do is keep preparing our hearts and minds for the work He has in store for us and continue to let Him teach us the things we need to learn."

"You're right. There's still so much of the Bible we haven't covered yet," LaMarcus said.

"Yep. But even when we're done looking at all the different books, it is essential that we always go back. There's always something new that God will show us every time we read the Bible, or perhaps even a new way of looking at something that we were already familiar with. It's absolutely important, LaMarcus, that we constantly feed ourselves with the Word of God. It's our only source of spiritual food in this lifetime.

Just as often as we need to eat earthly food daily to stay satisfied and full, we also must feed ourselves spiritually with the Word, daily. The consequence of not doing so is the same as if you don't eat earthly food: you become sick and are vulnerable to diseases."

"I understand, Mr. Curtis." LaMarcus said. Even though it was a tremendous responsibility to really study the Bible, LaMarcus couldn't help but be excited to read about what mystery Jesus would reveal next. It was over the course of the next several months, including going into the next year, that the real training and studying of the Word was about to begin.

CHAPTER 9

Later that same day, Mr. Curtis came walking back to the cell with a big smile on his face. He had been gone for a while, and he wasn't on any kind of special detail that LaMarcus was aware of. Nonetheless, he was ecstatic about something.

"What's got you all happy over there?" LaMarcus asked him.

"Oh, nothing much," Mr. Curtis answered. "I just got back from a meeting with the warden. I was able to convince him that the prison chaplain needed some extra help in reaching out to the other inmates, so he's agreed to create a detail to assist him. This way, the two of us can have an extra person in our study, and we can prepare ourselves to spread the Gospel, because that is indeed what we are supposed to be doing."

LaMarcus looked a little disappointed. "I kind of liked our one-on-one discussions. They were fun."

"Don't worry about that, LaMarcus," Mr. Curtis assured him. "We'll still have those, but it's a good thing to expand your groups as well. Every believer has something to add to the body of Christ that is beneficial to everyone else. Besides, you'll like the prison chaplain. He's a former pastor who's spent the latter portion of his life in prison ministry."

"Well, okay, if you say so," LaMarcus said.

"Good," said Mr. Curtis, "Because our first meeting with him is in an hour."

LaMarcus gave him a stare that seemed to say, "Why do you do things like that?" It didn't seem to matter to Mr. Curtis as he lied down on his bed and dozed off. LaMarcus shook his head. Even though he and Mr. Curtis were on the same page in a lot of things, he still had his moments where he was a little crazy. Maybe it was just his age showing. Who knew?

An hour later, right on cue, the guards came to take the two to the office of the prison chaplain. The office wasn't very big, but it had air conditioning, which is all the chaplain needed and something LaMarcus hadn't felt in months. It was very refreshing, actually. Sitting behind the desk was an elderly black man, not quite as old as Mr. Curtis, reading what appeared to be a Bible on his desk. Unlike Mr. Curtis, whose hair was mostly gray with a trace of its original color, this man still had most of his jet black hair intact with a few patches of gray in it.

When they walked in the room, the chaplain looked up at them and immediately greeted them. "Ah, welcome. Welcome. Please, come in. I got chairs for ya, sit on down here." Looking at the guards, he said, "Y'all can stand on outside the door now. We'll be okay in here for a good while." The guards gave him a motion of understanding and left the room, shutting the door behind them.

LaMarcus took note of the chaplain's voice. He had a very warm, joyful kind of voice to him. It was different from Mr. Curtis's voice in several ways. First, for whatever reason, maybe the tone or something, but there's always that sound you hear in a person's voice where you can tell a person's race without seeing them. But aside from that, Mr. Curtis had a much raspier kind of voice than this guy who just seemed to let words flow from him like a river.

"Ah, Mr. Curtis," he spoke again. "I was beginning to wonder if you'd ever come back and see me. I had such a good time with our Bible studies; I was beginning to miss them."

"Yeah, I'm sorry about that," Mr. Curtis said, "But I had to spend some time with this guy over here, teaching him some things about Jesus. And wouldn't you know it, he got saved just yesterday."

"Well, praise the Lord!" the chaplain exclaimed. "Once again, He has shown His faithfulness by bringing another one of His lost back home." Turning to LaMarcus, he said, "Welcome to the family and the body of Christ, young man."

Not really knowing how to respond, LaMarcus managed to muster up, "I really am grateful that Christ saved me. Now I want to learn everything I can so I can serve Him the right way."

"That's good to hear, young man. That's good to hear," said the chaplain. "And I take it that's why you brought him here, Mr. Curtis."

"Well, I figure learning from one experienced believer would be fine, but hearing from another would only help the boy. After all, we all bring something to the table, don't we?" Mr. Curtis said.

"That we do. That we do," the chaplain said. "Well, I'm very glad to have you here, and like Mr. Curtis, any knowledge I can pass on to you, I will be glad to do it."

Mr. Curtis turned to look at LaMarcus and said, "LaMarcus, I'd like you to meet Reverend Patrick, the prison chaplain."

"Pleased to meet you, sir," LaMarcus said.

"Likewise, young man," Mr. Patrick said.

"Mr. Curtis said you used to be a pastor before you came here. How come you left?" LaMarcus asked him.

"Simply put, I felt that this is where the Lord was calling me. I wasn't worried about my congregation. I knew the Lord would take care of them. Folks can easily replace a pastor. Shoot, the young man leading them now, the Lord had me train him ever since he was just a little tike. They're in good hands, for the Lord will always be with them. These people in here, they've never known God before, nor do they even begin to understand where they stand in this life or in the next. There are not many that are willing to listen, but I'll always be here for when they are. These people need me far more than the ones in my old church. That's why the Lord led me here."

After some more exchange in dialogue, in which they all talked about each other, Mr. Curtis suggested they go ahead and get started with the book of Acts, since that was the next book in line after the four Gospels. They read about the outpouring of the Holy Spirit on the apostles and all in the Upper Room on the Day of Pentecost. They read on about Stephen, the first martyr, and made mention about the importance of martyrdom and how all believers, though not all will experience it, are called to embrace it. Mr. Curtis promised that they would expand more on that topic someday, but he wanted to move on and discuss a Jewish man by the name of Saul. He was a Pharisee who set out on a mission to rid Israel of the growing Christian problem. He participated in the capture and execution of several Christians in the nation and was hailed a hero by the Jewish leaders.

One day on the road to Damascus, where he planned to slaughter many more Christians, a light shined in front of him, blinding him. A voice called out to him and revealed Himself to be Jesus. After being healed from his blindness three days later, Saul, whose name would later be changed to Paul, began to preach the very things that he once executed others for saying. The apostles, Jewish leaders, and peoples who knew him, were astonished to see him proclaim the things he once came against. Paul was chosen by God to be the apostle to the Gentiles and was sent to Asia Minor, Rome, Greece, and even Asia. He would go on to be the most famous of the apostles and wrote some of the most powerful letters to various churches which would become books in the New Testament.

"You see," Mr. Patrick continued, "It's in the rest of the book of Acts and in these letters that Paul, by the wisdom of the Holy Spirit, is able to clarify and even expand on the things that Jesus taught. Not excluding any of the books of the New Testament by any means, but it's in Paul's letters where you will find many of the teachings on how to live a life for Christ, a life like Christ, and so many other wonderful things. Seeing how the whole Bible is the Word of God, you can take just as much stock in Paul's words as you can Jesus's words, because every word in this book comes straight from the heart of God. That having been said, Jesus's words are the most precious to me because it's the Lord Himself speaking to His people. No matter which book of the Bible you read, really sit down, dissect it, diligently read it, and absorb what it has to say. Always take it seriously, no matter what you're studying." Mr. Patrick spoke with a serious voice, but ever still as warm and jolly as before.

"Paul must've really been something special," LaMarcus said. "Who would've thought that such an enemy to the Apostles would turn into such an ally?"

"And with such an extensive study in the Jewish Law, it only helped Paul further in his explanations of how Jesus had come and fulfilled it," Mr. Curtis added.

"Yep, the Lord taught him a lot. He mimicked Christ to the best of his ability with his preaching, his ministry, and even reprimanding the apostle Peter on one occasion," Mr. Patrick said. "If there's one person in the Bible I can relate to the most, it's Paul."

LaMarcus wondered what exactly he meant by that as the reverend continued.

"I remember back in my youth, oh, about when I was your age, I was a staunch atheist. I couldn't be convinced for anything that a living, loving God existed. I grew up in a bad spot in Birmingham, Alabama. I saw my family and my friends' families all living in shacks, poverty stricken, and felt like the world was against us. I'd see the cops hosing down black people in the streets, good people...people I knew. Hatred roamed the streets. The white people hated us, and we hated them for what they were doing. I thought to myself, *how could a loving God allow all this to happen?* I thought that if God were real, these things couldn't and wouldn't happen. So I thought that our lives couldn't be in the hands of God, but rather our lives were in our own hands, even the lives of unborn children."

Mr. Patrick continued. "I was incredibly naïve in my youth. I believed anything I heard that came against God and the Christians and what they believed, all because of my anger and bitterness towards God. And then one day, it all came to a head. I was on my way to the rallies in Washington D.C. outside the Supreme Court for the decision of Roe v. Wade. On the way there, I lost control of my car, and I had a real bad accident. I was more or less trapped in my car, but I was so broken down, I couldn't move anyway. I heard a voice saying, 'Joe. Joe.' I tried crying out for help. Instead of answering me, suddenly swarms of thoughts entered my mind. I was trapped and defenseless, fighting for life. In the midst of all the pain and agony I felt, I realized that before me was a similar picture of what an unborn child goes through moments before it is killed in the womb. After I was rescued and lying in the hospital, I began to picture all of those babies getting killed and it was horrifying to think about. It was then I started to consider what the Bible, said and the Lord showed me so much of myself and the world around me."

Lamarcus kept his eyes fixed on Mr. Patrick.

"The truth is that God never wanted these bad things to happen. We brought them on ourselves in our sin. But He still allows them to happen. He allows them to happen and lets the world get messed up to show everyone how mighty He is and how we can never make it on our own. I learned later in life, too, that I had it made in comparison to others around the world. The place that I called a shack, others would've called a mansion compared to what they had. I thought we were in poverty, but we were rich compared to them. Some of these communities that had it worse than me in one regard were much richer than I was. They had everything they needed, because they had come to know Christ. And I know God will continue to send missionaries to other places like them to share Christ. These people here though, I've been called to them. I've been where they're at, and I know about hatred. Unfortunately, in more recent years, they believe the hatred is just always there from the white people, and it is for some, but in many cases, it comes from their own minds and the delusions that Satan has put there. My goal is to help them understand that they must let go of their hatred and replace it with Jesus Christ."

LaMarcus had never heard another black man talk like this before, but what he said made sense. As a follower of Christ, he could not hold on to his general resentment of white people anymore. And what he said of others around the world really hit home. The ones who had less than him but had Christ, it turned out that they had more than him up until the previous day. LaMarcus made the determination in his mind that from now on, Jesus was going to be that kind of supplier to him. Like he would later read from Paul in Philippians, he knew that the only way to seriously follow Christ would be to count everything as worthless in comparison to knowing and following Christ.

"Not only did Paul give great teaching and understanding on how to live a Spirit-filled life," Mr. Curtis added, "Paul was a prime example of following Jesus's last and great commission to His disciples, which was in fact spreading the Gospel and making new disciples in all the nations. His boldness in the face of those who didn't believe him, even when he was in chains on multiple occasions, is the kind of boldness that we must allow the Holy Spirit to instill in us so that we can stand firm when presenting the Gospel."

"Amen, brother," Mr. Patrick said, and then looking at his watch, added, "Well, it looks like we've gone over today. Not that I like to put God in a box, but the warden may get upset if you're not back in your cell."

So with the session concluded for the day, the two men returned to their cells and talked even further about what was said. LaMarcus said, "You're right, I think I am going to like him. He's very good at this sort of thing. Almost as good as you are."

Mr. Curtis laughed. "Well, he has had his own share of experiences, and God has been with him through it all. He's been a real blessing to have while I've been here."

"I can imagine," LaMarcus said. "You want to start on Paul's letters then?"

"Tell you what, kid. Why don't you go ahead and read them yourself, and we can talk about them later. It'll be good for you to have some one-on-one time with the Lord. And I need a nap anyway."

"All right," LaMarcus said. "Sounds good to me." And while Mr. Curtis slept, LaMarcus sat down on his bed and began to read from the book of Romans and started applying what Mr. Patrick had said about diligently dissecting what was being said.

CHAPTER 10

R omans was a very difficult read for LaMarcus, at least in the early
parts of the book. The whole deal with circumcision being relevant
to salvation at first didn't make sense to him. But then he remembered
the old Jewish Law that called for all males to be circumcised. The issue
that Paul was debating with the Roman church was that circumcision was
only ever an outward showing of the inward obedience to the Law—
much like baptism is an outward expression of the change that occurs
in the heart when Jesus is given control. What Paul was arguing, though,
was that circumcision was in fact not a necessity to salvation, because the
observance of the Law was never a path to salvation. The Law made us
aware of sin, and it came from God, so it was a good thing. Knowing the
Law, however, prompted the human nature of the Jews to sin even more.

Perhaps this analogy will help explain. You are a child and your
parents have laid out a list of rules. They don't tell you why these rules
are important. They simply state that you are not to break them or else,
under their authority as your parents, they would be forced to punish
you. But you, as the child, especially in the teenage years, are left with
two choices: respect and obey your parents, or break the rules anyway
because you just want to do what you want to do. It's for this reason
that merely having the Law was not enough for salvation for the Jewish
people or really anyone for that matter. Something else would have to
save them, an act of grace, if you will.

Paul mentions in Romans 7 about his own struggle with his sinful
nature, wanting to do right but instead doing the things he hated. But it's

revealed at the end of the chapter that it is Jesus Christ who has rescued him from himself. And it is for that reason that at the start of Romans 8, he says, "Therefore, there is now no condemnation to any of them who are in Christ Jesus, who walk not after the flesh, but the Spirit."

Of course this was only the first half of the book. Paul not only defined where the saving power lied between the Law and grace through faith, but also talked about the ones who followed the Law, the Jews, and the ones who were being saved by grace through faith, mostly Gentile believers. LaMarcus took note of the special care and concern that Paul had for his fellow brethren. He reminded the church in Rome how the Jews, the descendants of Abraham through his son Isaac and his grandson Jacob, were God's chosen people. Paul taught that God had not cast away His people for the rejection of the Messiah. Like in Elijah's time, a remnant of Jews have come to know Christ, while the rest have been blinded to the Truth. The Jews have stumbled, yes, but it was of necessity to bring in the Gentiles and provoke them to jealousy. But all is not over for the Jewish people. Paul mentioned how their stumbling brought reconciliation to the world, and there would come a time of restoration for them. The restoration of the Jewish people would bring even more restoration to the world: as Paul put it, life from the dead.

LaMarcus then read Paul's warning to the Gentiles that they not think themselves above the Jews. He read that if God would cut off some of the natural branches from His olive tree, how much more then could the engrafted ones be cut off. It was a very steep warning to LaMarcus about letting the pride he had in his new status get the best of him. As he would later read in James and 1 Peter, "God stands against the proud, but gives grace to the humble." Paul also mentioned that one day the natural branches would be grafted back in themselves; not that God doesn't currently look at His people with His favor, but after the fullness of the Gentiles, in other words, when the last of the Gentiles who are to come to know Christ find him, the blinders will be removed from Israel, and all of Israel shall be saved. LaMarcus did his best to picture such a glorious day in which the longtime apple of God's eye would finally come to know that Jesus was their Messiah. Paul explained that though the Jews were enemies of the Gospel, they were still a part of the elect of God, and as such, were beloved to the Father who does not repent from those who He calls. Paul reminds us that we once did not believe, but now we have mercy, so we must show it to the Jews who now do not believe so that they may find mercy as God desired all to find it.

There is more to the book of Romans for sure, but many of the things Paul talks about in the final chapters are made mention of in other Epistles, so it would be best to move on so as to avoid redundancy.

LaMarcus then moved on to 1 Corinthians where Paul immediately talks about the ones who the world deems as foolish will make fools of them that call themselves wise. True wisdom comes from the Holy Spirit who teaches us the wisdom of God. He warned the Corinthian church of taking sides between the apostles: following them instead of Christ. He warned them about staying away from immorality, not even eating with one who commits such acts should it have an influence on them, and removing any such immorality that may try to infiltrate the church.

By the time LaMarcus reached the end of chapter 6, he was in for some major conviction. He began to read the warning against fornication of the body. The body is the temple for the Holy Spirit, and we, the members of the church, are the body of Christ. To fornicate ourselves, even to a harlot, is to do the same thing to Christ. Think of what sex really is. It's the consummation of marriage, or in other words, the marriage becoming official. Remember what God said the symbol of marriage was in Genesis: "the two shall become one flesh." LaMarcus realized that if you took that at face value, then every time a guy goes sleeping around with a bunch of girls, or vice versa, they are officially marrying themselves to them, since their bodies are becoming one flesh. In that regard, many would be violating the one man/one woman standard of marriage. If you add Christ living within someone who does that, it just makes it all the worse.

But just as in marriage the bodies become one, in a relationship with Christ, Paul revealed that your spirit becomes one with God's Spirit. It was here that LaMarcus began to grasp a fuller understanding of surrendering your life to Christ, as he read the final verses of the chapter. "Know you not that your body is a temple for the Holy Spirit, which is in you, which you have of God, and you are not your own? For you are bought with a price: therefore glorify God in your body and your spirit, which are God's."

And so, LaMarcus read on from the controversial chapter 7, in which many people believe Paul is coming against marriage, a God ordained thing, when in fact he is not. He continued to chapter 12, which discusses spiritual gifts, to chapter 13, one of the most important chapters Paul would ever write, and it concerned the importance of love. Paul discusses in great detail that if love is not the motive of your actions, then all of your actions are for nothing. It made sense to LaMarcus. He went back to that classic verse: John 3:16. What was God's motive for the grace in sending His Son? His love for the people He created. Were it not for that love, the Father would never have sent His own Begotten to the slaughter.

LaMarcus then read chapter 15, which talks profoundly of the resurrection of Christ. There was something else mentioned in this chapter that LaMarcus had heard Mr. Curtis make mention of before, but this was the first time he read it in the Bible. LaMarcus read how in the last days, the resurrected dead in Christ would gain new spiritual bodies—not bodies that would make them spirits or ghosts, but rather physical bodies that would be, for lack of better words, in better likeness to the second Adam, or rather Jesus Christ. It was a very interesting concept for LaMarcus and one he made note to do more investigating about. Even if it was to be in heaven, the idea of being a spirit, ghost type thing just floating around was one that made him uncomfortable. This, however, was something completely different.

The next day, this same kind of studying continued. LaMarcus read through 2 Corinthians, learning more about Paul's personal sufferings and his warning of false prophets and turning back to sin. In Galatians, he read about the fruits of the Spirit. In Ephesians, he studied more of how we are saved by grace through faith. He also learned about the armor of God, which contained the belt of truth, the breastplate of righteousness, the shoes of peace, the shield of faith, the helmet of salvation, the sword of the Spirit, which is the Word, and always being in prayer for the supplication of the saints.

In Philippians, LaMarcus read one of the most emphatic messages Paul would write about counting all as loss for Christ. Mr. Curtis explained to him that this was what Jesus meant when He told His disciples to deny themselves, pick up their cross, and follow him. This was indeed martyrdom, living a martyred life with the ultimate culmination of a martyred death.

Philippians 1:21 says, "To live is Christ and to die is gain." Mr. Curtis explained this verse this way: A person who comes to know Christ and gives up everything, counting it as loss, in place of knowing and walking in Him, this is a martyred life. A martyred life is the resultant fruit that one bears when they let Christ live in them, or rather through them. Letting Christ live through us is the only meaningful way to live, which is what Paul means when he says, "To live is Christ." But a martyred life is not truly a martyred life without the willingness to die. A martyred death is the greatest expression of the martyred life, because it is a sign to all that we followed Jesus even to the point of death. It is the greatest way to glorify God, and we can partake of joy because it brings God glory. It also then brings us into the very presence of God after we die. Though the presence of God is always with us through the Spirit, when we die, we will be able to see Jesus face to face. This is what Paul means when he says, "To die is gain."

"It's no wonder, then," Mr. Curtis told him, "that Paul found it a near impossible choice between life and death. In life, he had the chance to serve Christ, and in death, he would be with Christ. His resolve, though, set the precedent. While I am here, I will continue to be the benefit that these young Christians need and leave the decision of when my time comes to the Lord. And that is what we all must do. Only the Lord knows when our time is up and when He will call us home. Until then, all we can continue to do is serve Him in everything we do and continue to make new disciples."

After their second meal break for the day, they turned to the next of Paul's Epistles, which was Colossians. Most of Colossians, LaMarcus found, was repeating most of what Paul had said in previous letters, just maybe not said exactly the same. It was not any less important, however, and the idea that Paul's letters were very consistent in their themes served as a reminder to LaMarcus that what was being said was truth and must be taken seriously. Colossians' main focal point seemed to be removing the old man, and replacing it with the new man in Christ. Mr. Curtis explained that this was another way of looking at the core Christian doctrine of replacing the old/human/sinful nature with the new/godly/

Christ-like nature, no longer being in the flesh but being in the Spirit, no longer practicing sin, but practicing being like Christ. Mr. Curtis also told him another name for this self-denial change for the things of God, which would make it easier to draw back reference, and that name is, *the sanctification process.*

When it came time to read 1 and 2 Thessalonians, Mr. Curtis stopped him and said, "I'd like to hold on to those for another study, if that's okay with you."

LaMarcus looked up bewildered, and said, "Um, okay, sure. Any particular reason?"

"Well, there's a particular subject in those books that is a part of another subject found in most of the Bible. I would like to talk about it when we go back to some of the other books of the Bible we haven't looked at yet."

LaMarcus went along with it, but it got the wheels in his head turning. Any time before when Mr. Curtis had this kind of reaction, it always had some kind of big special meaning at the end when he would finally talk about it. Instead, they moved on to 1 and 2 Timothy. It was in these Epistles where Paul instructs how to be a good teacher and avoid the doctrines of demons. Second Timothy, which is believed to be Paul's final letter, based on 4:6-8, also warns once again of separating from the things of sin. For as Paul said, there will come a time when evil will greatly increase in the world, and if we are to make it without turning back to sin, we must hold on to the things that we have learned.

The book of Titus contained very similar things to that which Paul had written to Timothy. The book of Philemon, though a small, humble book, contains a rather profound example of forgiving one who did wrong. Paul was sending a man named Onesimus to Philemon, who was known for an unnamed wrong that Paul counted simply as being unprofitable to Philemon. Apparently, Paul spent a lot of time with that man, because he was now sending him back to Philemon with a changed heart. Paul so greatly interceded for this man that he told Philemon if by chance he should fall again, then put it on his (Paul's) account.

As Jesus once pointed out, if you go to someone, and they don't receive the Gospel, then shake the dust off your feet and move on. Here, this is a different case, for Onesimus was already a follower of Christ who was still warring with his old nature. For him and others like him, Paul is basically saying, "don't give up on these." These people are trying to grasp hold of what it means to have the power of God available to them, and we, as Christian brothers and sisters, must support and help them.

While Christ certainly does not want us to totally give up on those who don't accept Him, if they don't have ears to hear, then we simply move on to someone who will, and then on another day, try again. These who war in their minds between the natures already belong to Christ, and we are not to abandon them, because Christ would not. Much like the shepherds of old who would chase after the sheep who left the flock, this is the same attitude Christ has with His sheep, and by Him living through us, He will go after His sheep. And we as fellow sheep simply cannot allow ourselves to hold spite at the ones who run away and must be chased down and led back to the herd.

This sort of diligent study, which when reading the Old Testament had been practiced to a degree, was applied now every time LaMarcus and Mr. Curtis would study. It could be recorded also, their studies of Hebrews and the Epistles of James, Peter, John, and Jude, which you can bet were also studied with great severity. However, it would be wise to take the time to read these fine books of the Bible yourself. It may be possible that the bigger picture of what LaMarcus learned may then be revealed.

After the reading of all these New Testament books, the pair went back to the Old Testament and started covering the books they hadn't read, or only read parts of. Now that LaMarcus had the end picture of Jesus in mind, understanding the old Jewish writings came much easier. So much was focused on the nation of Israel, which of course made sense, as they were the ones who would bring forth the Messiah to the world. And it was because of this Israel-centric focus that the concerns of Paul from Romans 11 began to take even stronger meaning in LaMarcus's heart. Thinking on the things he learned from that chapter while reading Israel's history created a level of gratefulness and responsibility to the Jewish people. Since then, LaMarcus, to this day, always remembers Israel in his prayers and has given them a special place in his heart. Oh, if only all who called themselves Christians had this same passion for these precious people.

CHAPTER 11

I n the midst of their studies of Paul's letters, LaMarcus had a burning question on his mind that he just couldn't keep down anymore. When they had met with Mr. Patrick, he had almost immediately shared his background with him. While LaMarcus enjoyed listening to his testimony, he later realized that he didn't even really know the background of the very one who led him to Christ, Mr. Curtis. It really began to eat at his curiosity. Even before he got saved, LaMarcus always thought that it didn't make sense for someone like him to be locked away in here. What did he do? How was it that he came to know Christ?

LaMarcus never had the chance to ask him, however , because, as if it was an act of God, Mr. Curtis said to him, "You know what I just thought of? Mr. Patrick gave such a wonderful testimony the other day, and come to think of it, I don't believe I've ever shared mine with you."

LaMarcus grinned. *The Lord works in mysterious ways*, he thought.

"Well, while I don't have a near death conversion story like Mr. Patrick, at least I can say that once I was lost, but now I am found in Jesus. I grew up in a Christian home. I came to know Jesus, because I saw the joy He brought to members of my family, and I knew deep down that it was a decision I had to make. In my late teenage years though, I began to develop what those know-it-all psychiatrists would call a self-destructive pattern. I began to live for myself, not giving two cares about the God that I had pledged my allegiance to. I spiraled down into some dark, hateful times: suicidal thoughts were a constant.

"Then one day, God got a hold of me. I remember thinking back on the times when I was serving Christ. I never really liked myself at any point, even back then, but I thought at least I was in a right standing with him. So I began to turn everything back over to the Lord and really study the Scriptures. It's really easy to learn about the Lord as a child. You learn all of the stories, and you're told to obey Jesus just like you would your parents. A child becoming saved is a marvelous display of maturity and work by the Holy Spirit. And it is because of the renewing of the mind that Jesus tells us to come to Him as having the minds of little children so that He may teach us through the Spirit. A child-like mind obeys Jesus's teachings because they are supposed to, but where the Spirit longs to bring our minds into maturity is in making Him Lord.

"When you make Jesus your Lord, you go from the mind of doing these things because you're supposed to, to doing these things because you want to. Though we come to Him with child-like minds, this is a concept that is easier for adults, not all mind you, to understand than children. As a child, I followed Christ to a degree because I wanted to, but it was more because I knew that He was God, and I was supposed to. Now as an adult, I finally began to realize the maturity that the Holy Spirit had tried to instill in me even when I was a child. Now, I wanted to follow Christ. I wanted to make Him not just my path to salvation, but also my Lord. It goes along with what we have been discussing in Paul's letters. Isn't it an irony that, by submitting yourself to the lordship of Christ, you find freedom from sin—that freedom being in Christ? There is freedom in surrender: a concept that could only come from God and only makes sense with Jesus."

"If you've been saved your whole life, then how did you end up in here?" LaMarcus asked.

"As I grew up, I began of course to preach the Gospel to people, something that I shall continue to do until I die. But more and more so, the Lord began to put a responsibility on my heart to straighten out people who are of a religious sort. They follow a God they don't even really know, with access to life-changing power in that same God, and they put their light under a bushel. Their hearts are callous and their lives are carnal. Different people had different spirits, and different churches had different problems, but it all pointed back to religion. The battles I fought with those religious spirits, as you can see, have taken a toll on me. I am hated by those that I call mediocre Christians."

LaMarcus kept his eyes on Mr. Curtis as he continued speaking. "And in the ever wonderful, self-righteous, politically correct, arrogant society we live in, I have also been heavily attacked by those who don't believe. I've been told I fringe on others' rights. I've been told that I force God down on people's throats. I've been told that I spread hate, and am myself a bigot. I've been told that I spread lies, that I'm racially, culturally, and sexually insensitive. I've been told many things, and I have suffered many things." Mr. Curtis paused for a moment. "I have lost my home—it was burned to the ground. I have lost all my money and all my possessions, save my Bible and my radio. I have been beaten in the streets and in prison more times than I can count. I have lost close friends. They were murdered by politicians in cold blood and in broad daylight among a sea of people, chanting and cheering them on, and though the police and lawyers witnessed it, they were never arrested and brought to trial. I have been flogged, water-boarded, burned, and tortured in unspeakable ways. And yet I still feel that to this day, all my sufferings have been light in comparison to my fellow brothers across the world and even in times past, like the apostles, and certainly light in comparison to my Master."

"Simply put," Mr. Curtis said, "any time I have been arrested, it has been for preaching the Gospel anywhere I went, from the shadiest of street corners to the most luxurious of buildings, and renouncing the spirits of religion that have infiltrated the church, save but one time. Once I was arrested for refusing to pay my taxes. I did this in protest to the city's ordinance that over half of the paid taxes from the city's citizens would go to funding a local Islamic rights organization. I was not about to let the money that God had given me be given over to the agenda of Satan. So instead, I went to jail, and they seized my assets. I have never owned a home or had money in my pocket since then, but it doesn't bother me one bit."

"I don't understand, though. How can they just arrest you for preaching the Gospel? We have freedom of religion and speech and assembly," LaMarcus said.

"We don't have those rights nearly to the capacity as we once had them. While it seems at times you are antagonized for speaking against the government, the bottom line is that it goes far beyond that. It is a battle between light and darkness. The darkness can't stand the light and is doing everything to purge it. That is why the name of Jesus is such an offense to all who walk in darkness. Jesus is the Truth. He is the Light. The light that He shines into darkness is the truth, and that very light and truth is what dispels the darkness. Remember, Jesus did not come to bring peace, but a sword. That sword is not a physical sword to fight a physical war, but it is the sword of the Spirit, brought to fight a spiritual war. It is meant to divide those that follow the light, and those that follow the darkness. The world is trying to remove Jesus from itself. However, it has already tried to once before, and it failed miserably when Jesus rose from the dead. The same result will be had in this case. The world will eventually remove Jesus to the point that any preaching or assembly for the purpose of spreading His name will be punished by death. It will seem as though Jesus will be truly expunged from the world, but then all their efforts will be in vain on the day that Jesus returns in glory. And on that day, 'every knee will bow and every tongue will confess that Jesus Christ is Lord.'"

"I see," said LaMarcus. "But I have one other question. Why would it matter if your money went to an Islamic group? Aren't they serving the same God but just with slightly different beliefs?"

"Oh, no, LaMarcus. They do not serve the same God that we do." Mr. Curtis spoke in a very grave voice. "And even if they did, why should I honor a religion that believes different from what the Bible teaches? The Lord is not inconsistent in His teachings. He warns in the book of Revelation not to take away or add to the Scriptures, which are the Word of God. All religions of the world, even religions that claim to be Christian in nature like Mormons, Jehovah's Witnesses, and Catholicism, add to and take away from the Bible. The Bible, which is the old Law of the Hebrews fulfilled in the new covenant made by Jesus, is the only Word of God, and I will go to the Lord not believing any differently."

Mr. Curtis continued. "Don't misunderstand me on one thing though, LaMarcus. Just because I find fault with these religions doesn't mean that I hate the people who practice them. The people are ignorant of their foolishness. They are not the enemy. Satan, who is manipulating them through these religions, he is the enemy. I love these people as

Christ loves them. I will lay down my life if it means that these people will come to know Jesus. Even the Muslims who have nothing but hatred for me because of Jesus, I desire them to know the Truth because we are all God's creations. But the thing is, if I love them with the love of Christ, then I have to tell them the truth: the religion they are practicing is wrong. When Jesus said to pick up our crosses, He didn't follow up with, 'follow my religion.' He said, 'follow me.' That is what everyone, no matter their background, must come to accept."

LaMarcus sat, deeply intrigued by the things Mr. Curtis was saying.

"The spirit of religion, no matter which religion, is one of, if not the most difficult spirit to face. We must remember that the people are not the enemy, but rather they are the reason that we fight for their souls by the power of Jesus. At the same time, however, we must understand that religions are strongholds. Religions and religious spirits are enemies of God and we must recognize them as such. Such is the case with Islam. I love the Arab people. They are descendants of Ishmael, whose very name means 'God hears.' The Arab people, though not the promised heirs, are still a special people to God, and He longs to see them come to him. They are, however, held in a deep bondage named Islam and it is only with speaking the truth in love that they will ever see they need Jesus. Without Jesus, they will never find their way to the Father, who they so long to worship. As Paul warned, we must be wary of the wiles of the devil. The best way to do this is to know Jesus. Once we know who He is, we can recognize the counterfeit. But Jesus also spoke directly of the tactics of Satan, and without giving Satan unnecessary attention, we can learn and know how He operates. It is important to learn how the enemy works so that we will be able to guard ourselves in Christ. One day, LaMarcus, we will have great discussions about Islam and the challenge it poses to the church. You will then begin to understand the gravity of our times. Remember, once again, that when you uncover the dark nature of Islam, you don't hate the people who practice it. This is a concept that must be understood."

Then, a thought from the Spirit came on LaMarcus. He turned to Mr. Curtis and said, "Love the sinner and hate the sin."

Mr. Curtis nodded, and then they continued from where they had left off in their reading.

CHAPTER 12[1]

S ome weeks or so later, after they had finished the Epistles, Mr. Curtis told LaMarcus to get ready for a really long series of studies. They would be looking at many Old Testament books they had previously skipped and also some from the New Testament.

"Mr. Curtis, do these studies have anything to do with why we skipped over 1 and 2 Thessalonians?" LaMarcus asked him.

"Yes, they do," Mr. Curtis answered. "What we're going to do is study one giant topic in the Bible that we have mentioned from time to time, but never really discussed it. You see, LaMarcus, everything that is written in the Bible is centered around two things: Jesus's First Coming as the sacrificial Lamb, and His Second Coming as the glorified King. There are three different subjects of literature used to promote these two important events within the Bible: history, moral/Christ-like living—which is needed to be learned in act of preparation for the Second Coming—and finally, prophecy. Unfortunately, for most within the church, prophecy is the one that they like to shy away from, at least as it pertains to the Second Coming of Christ and the last days. No one has a problem reading the prophecies about the First Coming of Christ, but

---

1   Positions on end times and prophecy presented in chapter twelve and chapter thirteen were taken based on the following sources: Joel Richardson, *Islamic Antichrist* (Los Angeles: WND Books, 2009); Joel Richardson, *Mideast Beast* (Washington D.C.: WND Books, 2012); Marv Rosenthal, *The Pre-wrath Rapture* (Nashville: Thomas Nelson Inc., 1990).

all passages of Scripture that pertain to end-time prophecy, the church generally avoids like taboo."

"Why?" LaMarcus asked. "I mean, that doesn't really make sense, does it? It's in the Bible, so obviously God thought it was important to share with His people."

"I know, right?" Mr. Curtis said. "Unfortunately, Satan has been allowed to cloud people's minds in this area so that many feel it just too controversial or too hard to understand, or these passages don't apply to them because they don't feel they'll be here for one reason or another. The fact of the matter is not only is it important to study these passages because, as you said, they are in the Bible for a reason, but the Lord commanded His disciples to know the signs of the times. There are just as many if not more passages about the Second Coming than there are about the First Coming. To not understand and talk about prophecy concerning the end times is to have a distorted partial Gospel."

Mr. Curtis continued. "When Jesus began His ministry, He preached on what He called the Gospel of the kingdom. In the past, the Israelites thought the Messiah would come and both liberate and reestablish the kingdom of Israel. This is true to a degree, but when Jesus returns, He will not only reestablish the kingdom of Israel, but He will also build an even greater kingdom with it, His kingdom. His kingdom will be one that will reconcile heaven and earth to Him, and in Him, heaven and earth shall be one."

"And when He sets up His kingdom, is that when we receive our resurrected bodies like Paul talked about?" LaMarcus asked.

"Just before, actually, if my understanding is correct," replied Mr. Curtis. "Before Jesus sets up His kingdom, He will first purge the earth of all unrighteousness. This is part of a major prophetic event called the Day of the Lord. The prophets and apostles speak of this day throughout the Bible—the prophets so much so that most of their words center around this great and terrible day."

"How is it both great and terrible?" LaMarcus asked.

"It is great because the Lord will return and execute the long awaited justice on the unrighteous. As Isaiah and many of the other prophets foretold, it will be a day of vindication for the nation of Israel. For these same reasons, it will also be terrible. It will be the ultimate day of God's wrath. The prophet Joel described it like this: 'The Day of the Lord is great and very terrible and who can abide it?' Other translations say, 'Who can withstand it?' He describes it as a day of great darkness, not the evil kind of darkness, but darkness that stems from the fear and terror the people will receive when standing before the face of a very angry God. Isaiah talks of the robes that Jesus will wear being scarlet red from the blood of all those who die on the Day of the Lord. According to Isaiah, saints will ask Him why His clothes are red as one who treads in the winepress. Jesus will answer, 'Because I tread it alone. No one was with me.' Now, this is not a word of condemnation on the part of the Lord. No one treads it with Jesus, because Jesus is the only one who can enact this kind of vindication. No longer do we have to fight. The Lord will be physically present on the earth, fighting for us. This will be the time when believers see a rare but very real side to our God, and that is a side of holy justice and vengeance."

"I have a question, though. How is it that believers won't feel the effects of His vengeance? Even if it is not directed at them, would they not live on in a broken world?"

Mr. Curtis looked disappointed. "Now, LaMarcus, what have I told you a thousand times? Don't get ahead of God. There are a million things to discuss, for even as the Day of the Lord is a sign for the kingdom of God, there are signs that we must look at that precede the Day of the Lord. Do me a favor and open up to 2 Thessalonians chapter 2. Start reading when you get there."

LaMarcus did as he was told and began reading: "Now we beseech you brothers, by the coming of our Lord Jesus Christ, and by our gathering to Him, that you be not soon shaken in mind, or be troubled, neither by spirit, nor by word, nor by letter as from us, as that the day of Christ is at hand. Let no man deceive you by any means: for that day shall not come, except there come a falling away first, and the man of sin be revealed, the son of perdition; Who opposes and exalts Himself above all that is called God, or that is worshipped; so that He as God sits in the temple of God, showing Himself that He is God." LaMarcus stopped reading after this and looked up at Mr. Curtis. "Who is this man of sin? Is it Satan?"

"No, not Satan, but one who will come representing him and will be given power by Satan. This is not the first mention of him. The prophets all spoke of him. And believe me, we will look at all of the end time passages. But to give you some more of His names, He is the man of lawlessness, the man of sin, the son of perdition, the beast, the little horn, the king of the north, the Assyrian, Gog of Magog, or as he is most commonly known, the Antichrist."

LaMarcus shivered at the thought of such a being. Someone who was just as evil as Christ was good didn't sit too well with him. Mr. Curtis was quick to cut off his thoughts.

"Don't think for one second to compare the two as on the same playing field. The Antichrist is indeed evil, sold to Satan, but he does not hold the power that Jesus holds. The prefix *anti* does not mean opposite so much here as it means false. In other words, this person intends to deceive people, pretending to be Christ, but know now that when Jesus returns, He will overthrow him and cast him into the lake of fire."

Mr. Curtis explained that the proper way to study about the Antichrist, or any of the prophetic Scriptures for that matter, was to start early in the Old Testament. He noted that many irresponsibly start with the book of Revelation or even Daniel, but these books build upon and include things that are repeated in other books. To get the full picture, all of the passages must be read and understood. Much like the four accounts of the Gospel, the easiest way to look at end time prophecy is to understand that all of the prophets are telling the exact same story but some with different perspectives and some with more details than others.

"It is important," he told LaMarcus, "that as we realize all the prophets tell the same story, we then realize we must study the text as one story. For example, as we study the Antichrist, in conjunction we must also study the Day of the Lord. The two go hand in hand. The final seven years prior to the Lord's kingdom is a time when the Antichrist comes to power, and it is at the Day of the Lord where he meets his end. That having been said, the Day of the Lord and what the Messiah will do on that day has been foretold by the prophets longer than that of even the revealing of the Antichrist."

Mr. Curtis then gave LaMarcus a list of passages to read. They were from Numbers 24, Isaiah 25, Isaiah 34, Isaiah 63, Ezekiel 25, Ezekiel 30, Joel 3, Zephaniah 2, and the book of Obadiah. After reading for what seemed like an eternity, Mr. Curtis asked him if he could remember the specific people that the Messiah would judge and crush at the Day of the Lord.

"Well, I know Moab was mentioned a lot," LaMarcus said, "and Edom, and I recognized Egypt and Libya. There were a lot of names that I think I've read about before, but they still seemed strange to me."

"Don't sweat it, kid. You did good to remember those after all that reading. Now, let me ask you something. The Lord seemed pretty serious about what He was going to do in those passages, didn't he?"

"Yeah, He did," LaMarcus said. "And it's like we talked about before. When Jesus returns, he'll vindicate Israel."

"Yes, that's right. In fact, He will judge all the nations based on their treatment of Israel as well. But these territories specifically, He has a real grudge against. It's because these are the worst of the worst in their treatment of Israel. Now, obviously, some time has passed since these prophecies were made. Do you think all of these territories are allegories or references to other nations, or do you think that the descendants of these territories will receive the same judgment prophesied on their ancestors, because they have continued in the same treatment of Israel?"

"Well, it sounded to me like the Lord had specific grievances towards these people. That, I guess, could be meaning other nations, but with such a passion against Moab and Edom, it sounds to me that He has to be talking to very specific people; that can't just mean anybody. So if their descendants are just as bad as they are, then yeah, I would say it would have to be those same people just in modern times."

Mr. Curtis smirked at him. "You're a smart kid, LaMarcus. Now would you like to learn the approximate locations of these territories?" After LaMarcus gave a nod of approval, he continued. "All of these different territories are located in modern day Jordan, Syria, Lebanon, Iran, Iraq, Saudi Arabia, Egypt—obviously—Libya, Sudan, and Turkey."

LaMarcus's eyes became really wide. "And all of those nations surround Israel, don't they? Then their location would make sense of their treatment of Israel."

"Their location is only part of the equation, LaMarcus. There is also their heritage. Can you figure out the one thing that all of these nations have in common with each other besides their hatred for Israel?" LaMarcus shook his head. "It's simple. They are all Islamic nations, and the Arab people, who are the main partakers of Islam, are all under the lineage of…"

"Ishmael!" LaMarcus blurted out.

"That's right. As we will see when we examine Islam, one of the main doctrines taught to Muslims is that Ishmael and not Isaac is the promised heir. Ever since Ishmael was removed from the camp, a hatred was built that has been passed from generation to generation. It was a hatred for his father, Abraham, and for his brother Isaac. The other of the main doctrines that Islam teaches is that God is not a father and that He has no son. This teaching stems from the resentment that Ishmael built inside of him. It was passed down to the enemies of Israel all throughout history and culminated in Israel's greatest enemy, the religion of Islam, which was created by a man named Muhammad who believed himself to be a direct descendant of Ishmael."

"Wow," LaMarcus thought. "You know when you think about it, it's sad. Even though the Jews are the chosen people, the Arabs are still their family. I mean, they all came from Abraham."

"You're right, it is sad," Mr. Curtis agreed. "But remember God's promise to both Abraham and Hagar? He promised to make Ishmael a great nation as well, and when you look at the Arab world today, I would say they are indeed a great nation in size, but I believe there is more. In my youth, I travelled to Israel, and many of the Arab believers believe that it will be them who provoke Israel to jealousy. They believe a great revival will break out among the descendants of Ishmael. I hope so as well for their sakes as well as the sakes of the Jews. Not all will decide to follow Christ, unfortunately. One day, they will see how wrong they have been. The Bible says that Israel's enemies will pay tribute to her and bring her gifts after Jesus establishes His kingdom. What a glorious sight that will be. Unfortunately, not all understand the gravity of identifying these territories correctly."

"What do you mean?" LaMarcus asked.

"There are some, many in fact, that believe these names to be references to other nations, namely unnamed European nations."

"Well, that doesn't make any sense," said LaMarcus. "I mean, those territories were in those places when the prophecies were written, so why would they be anywhere else when they are fulfilled?"

"That's a very good question, LaMarcus. They have their reasons for thinking so, and it will become clearer as we study. It will also become easier to classify the two sides after we take a heavy look at one of the most important prophecy books of the Bible, the book of Daniel."

CHAPTER 13[2]

B efore discussing anything else, Mr. Curtis told LaMarcus to read Daniel 2 and then immediately read Daniel 7. Here is what these two chapters discuss: Daniel 2 shows King Nebuchadnezzar, the ancient king of Babylon, receiving a dream. It was a dream that shook him to the very core, and he ordered his "wise" scribes and scholars to tell him both the dream, since he could not remember it, as well as the meaning. When they could not give him the meaning, the king ordered the execution of all his wise men. When Daniel, a Hebrew captive who had been placed in the service of the king, heard of this, he arranged an audience to meet with King Nebuchadnezzar. He asked the king to give him time to pray to his God for the revealing and meaning of the dream.

God honored Daniel's prayer and showed him both the dream and its interpretation. When Daniel returned to the king, he recited perfectly the king's dream. The king had seen a vision from God, which was of a "multi-metaled" statue, if you will. The head was made of gold, the chest and arms of silver, the mid-section and thighs of bronze, the legs of iron, and the feet partly of iron and partly of clay. After seeing all of this, a stone was then carved without human hands and it hurled toward the statue, striking it at the feet. When it connected at the feet, the whole

---

2   Positions on end times and prophecy presented in chapter twelve and chapter thirteen were taken based on the following sources: Joel Richardson, *Islamic Antichrist* (Los Angeles: WND Books, 2009); Joel Richardson, *Mideast Beast* (Washington D.C.: WND Books, 2012); Marv Rosenthal, *The Pre-wrath Rapture* (Nashville: Thomas Nelson Inc., 1990).

statue shattered, and the wind carried the pieces away, never to be seen again. As for the stone that struck the statue, it remained and became a great mountain that filled the whole earth.

Daniel then began to interpret the dream for the king. The head of gold represented King Nebuchadnezzar himself and through him the Babylonian Empire. Daniel explained that the other sections were kingdoms that were to follow the Babylonian Empire. The stone that destroyed the statue represented the kingdom of heaven that would cut down the kingdom of iron mixed with clay, thus destroying all those that came before, and this new kingdom of God's would stand forever.

Now this is a summary of Daniel 7: Daniel receives a vision of four beasts: the first, a winged lion; the second, a lopsided bear; the third, a four headed leopard; and the fourth is unnamed, but it had great crushing power, and out of this beast were ten horns. As Daniel is looking at the horns, another horn begins to grow in the midst of them and practically uproots three of the horns. What is so strange about it, Daniel finds, is that this new little horn had eyes like a man and a mouth speaking great things. Eventually, this beast was slain and thrown into the lake of fire. After this, the other beasts lost their dominion but were allowed to live for a season while their dominions, as well as the dominion of the fourth beast, were given to one like a son of man riding in the clouds to the judgment seat of the Ancient of Days. This dominion would never pass away, and the kingdom would never be destroyed.

Daniel was so greatly disturbed by everything that, in the vision, he asks someone for interpretation. It is explained to him that the four beasts are four great kingdoms of the earth. Daniel desired to learn more about the fourth beast and the horns. The interpreter, presumably an angel, explained that the fourth beast was the fourth kingdom which would devour the whole earth and break it into pieces. The ten horns represented ten kings that would arise from this empire. After these kings arise, another will arise, different from all the rest, and will subdue three of his fellow kings. This individual would speak great words against the Most High and shall wear out the saints of the Most High who will be given into his hand for a time, times, and half a time. But in the end, his kingdom shall be taken away and he along with it consumed. Though knowing the ultimate victory belonged to the people of God, Daniel was still greatly troubled by the actions of this person and his kingdom, but the last verse states that he kept the matter to himself.

When LaMarcus had finished reading, he looked up at Mr. Curtis with a mixed reaction. There were parts of his face that showed panic, but most was unadulterated confusion. Mr. Curtis just laughed at him.

"So, you lost yet?"

"Um, very much so," LaMarcus said. "Even after hearing the interpretations, I still don't get it."

"Did you notice anything similar in the two visions?" Mr. Curtis asked him.

LaMarcus thought about it for a minute. "Well, each of the sections of the metallic statue were kingdoms, and the beasts were kingdoms."

"That's right. These two visions are telling the same prophetic story of the same four great empires across the history of the earth. We know the head of gold to be the kingdom of Babylon, as Daniel revealed, and the prophet Jeremiah once referred to King Nebuchadnezzar as a 'lion from the thickets of Jordan.' We could spend more time proving this, but you're okay, right, with the head of gold and the first beast being Babylon?"

"Yeah. If it's telling the same story, it makes sense."

"Very well, then. The next two empires are the Medo-Persian Empire and the Greek Empire. The Medo-Persian Empire is confirmed in the book of Daniel with the invasion of Babylon after Belshazzar did profane things with the holy artifacts from the Jewish temple. They are later reconfirmed in other chapters of Daniel along with the mention of the Greek Empire. We can see in history that the Greek Empire did succeed the Medo-Persian Empire, and very specifically conquered the lands that were a part of its empire, much like the Medo-Persian Empire had done to Babylon.

"So the chest and arms of silver and the lopsided bear represent the Medo-Persian Empire. This can especially be seen in the lopsided bear. The Medes and Persians had come together to form this empire, but the Persians were far more powerful than the Medes, hence why the bear is portrayed as lopsided. Next, the midsection and thighs of bronze and the four headed leopard are the Greek Empire. Some translations read this metal as brass instead of bronze. Either way, the Greek army was famous for the use of bronze and brass in their thick armor and shields. The four heads on the leopard foretell of the four territory split of the Greek Empire after Alexander the Great suddenly died.

"Now the fourth beast is where things get interesting. The legs, if you remember, are of iron. The fourth beast has iron teeth. They are the same kingdom as well. This kingdom is seen as crushing, devouring, and trampling all in its path. It was a kingdom designed for one thing: complete annihilation and destruction of all who were not a part of it. This is where there is division among the church. Many believe this empire to be the Roman Empire. After all, Rome was practically next in line after the Greeks. They were in power when Christ was crucified. Crucifixion was of Roman origin to the core: not just an execution, but one bathed in humiliation."

LaMarcus interrupted him. "If the common belief is that it's Rome, then what's the problem?"

"I'll have to show you the maps the next time we are in Mr. Patrick's office," Mr. Curtis said. "But the problem is that when you really read and examine the text, the Roman Empire doesn't match the biblical description. The Roman Empire captured some of the territory these other empires had, but it never crushed the whole of these other empires, stomping on them without a trace. The Roman Empire was brutal in stopping rebellions, but it was more constructive. They allowed the Jews to practice their religion as long as they paid taxes to Caesar. They were known for building roads and mixing cultures. The iron kingdom seeks to eliminate everything that is not a part of it so that it is the only influence and force in the world. Yet many still believe this kingdom to be the Roman Empire and thus the Antichrist's kingdom a revived version of it."

"The Antichrist's kingdom? The iron kingdom is the Antichrist's kingdom?"

"No, not his kingdom. His will be a revived version of it, but it won't be as powerful. The feet of the statue is iron mixed with clay. It is a kingdom with traces of its predecessor, but the clay makes it not as strong. It's moldable if you will. Much like the feet, the ten horns are ten kings that arise after the fourth beast has had great dominion. It is here in Daniel 7 that the personage of the Antichrist is revealed as the little horn who emerges from this beast, but considerably later.

"As further proof that Rome is not the iron empire, there is a passage in the book of Revelation that talks of eight empires. While the empires mentioned in Daniel are four great massive empires, these empires contain both these great empires and also some lesser empires. These are empires in their respective times of reign that were great enemies of the nation of Israel, and in fact subdued her; not the nation of Israel as in Jews spread throughout the world, but very specifically the Hebrew people, the Israelites, in the land of promise. When John wrote of these, he wrote, 'five were, one is, and one will be.' In speaking of the eighth he said that it once was, but now is not. He reveals that it is of the seventh and will go to destruction. This is the kingdom of the Antichrist. The eighth empire is a copy of the seventh. As such, it can be said that the seventh like the eighth once was, but now is not, because the eighth is taken out of the seventh.

"Notice John also said that one is. One of the empires he was referring to was currently in power at the time he wrote the book. The five previous empires were Egypt, Assyria, Babylon, Medo-Persia, and Greece. At the time John wrote Revelation, Rome was in power. Therefore Rome is the one that is, and is the sixth. It can't be the seventh as well and be revived as the eighth. Many ignore the eighth empire and say the seventh is a revived version of Rome to force their revived Roman Empire and consequently European Antichrist doctrine into the Bible. But there are eight, and the fact that Rome was already in power at the time of the writing, goes to show that the seventh must be someone else."

"All right, so if not Rome, then who?" LaMacus asked.

"Who else do you know that has been a great grievance to the nation of Israel and has occupied its land?"

LaMarcus thought and said, "Well, I know the Arab people have a history with them, but…" He stopped when he saw Mr. Curtis nodding his head in approval. "But wouldn't it be one specific people or nation?"

"Not necessarily. There have been a series of Islamic dynasties that have consistently been in power since the sixth century and lasted until the early twentieth century. The Islamic Empire matches the description perfectly. Islam seeks to purge and remove anything that is not a part of itself. When Islamic nations conquered other peoples, they did so in a vicious fashion, mercilessly crushing their enemies. After they had conquered, they sought to remove any trace of the culture of the people that came before. The ultimatum for all infidels in the eyes of Muslims is to convert to Islam or die. There is no gray area. And if we were to look at maps, clearly the Islamic Empire dominated the lands once held by the Babylonian, Medo-Persian, and Greek Empires. And if this view is true, then even greater implications are brought into light. This view then means that the revived Islamic Caliphate would then be the Antichrist's power. Now compare the region of an Islamic Antichrist Empire to the nations that will be judged and crushed by Jesus at His return. It lines up perfectly, does it not?"

LaMarcus marveled at the idea. Yes, indeed, it made perfect sense. The history, the prophecy, it all interconnected. Mr. Curtis explained that the other prophets confirmed the Middle Eastern identity of the final end-times leader as the Jews have believed for centuries. Micah 5 refers to him as "the Assyrian." One of the most obvious was found in Ezekiel 38 and 39. This is the same story as the other prophets but from a very generalized overhead sort of view. In this, God is addressing a person named Gog from the land of Magog. He will raise up an army against Jerusalem, and it lists several peoples who will join him in his empire. Mr. Curtis revealed that five of these peoples came from what is now Turkey, and the others came from surrounding regions that today are Islamic.

"It's no surprise to see these five peoples once lived in Turkey. It is consistent with Micah's reference to the Antichrist in the name of 'the Assyrian.' The Assyrian Empire stretched as far north as the region of Asia Minor, which is Turkey. It is highly likely that the Antichrist will come from Turkey, or if not Turkey, the Turkish, Syrian, possibly northern Iraq area. Many still hold on to this passage as having nothing to do with the Antichrist at all because of their insistence to hold on to a European Antichrist. The passage even points out several things pertaining to the end. God looks at Gog and says, 'Are you not the one of whom all the prophets spoke?' After the Gog invasion, no longer will there be war, nor will Israel be shamed, nor the name of the Lord be profaned. After the invasion and Gog is defeated, the Lord holds a great feast. There is only one other place in the whole Bible that talks of a great feast at the table of the Lord. It is in Revelation after the defeat of the Antichrist."

LaMarcus was just beside himself, hearing how all of this was coming together. What really amazed him was the sheer arrogance and ignorance of people who claim Gog is another beside the Antichrist, when God Himself calls him out as being the same person that the other prophets spoke of, who in those passages are clearly talking of the Antichrist. *What are these people, stupid?* LaMarcus thought.

"There is one other controversial issue that we must discuss pertaining to the end times," Mr. Curtis said. "The final seven years of the age of man are described as Daniel's seventieth week in the Bible. At the start of these seven years, Israel will enter into a covenant of peace with the Antichrist for seven years, not knowing who he is or that the covenant that they have made is one of death. Half-way into the seven years, the Antichrist will break the treaty, setting up an abomination, which causes desolation. It is when he does this that his identity will be known to both the Jews and Christians who have studied the Word of God. After he does this, he will begin a grand persecution of the people of God. In Matthew 24, Jesus described it as a time of great tribulation, such as the world has never seen nor ever will see again. Thus this time in history is known as the Great Tribulation. It is a time of great peril for the saints that will last for three and a half years. This is what is mentioned in Daniel 7 with the phrase, 'time, times, and half a time.' Jesus teaches us, however, that this time would be cut short for the sake of the elect, lest all should fall from the faith. This grand day of deliverance is the same day that has been predicted for thousands of years."

"The Day of the Lord!" LaMarcus shouted, getting excited.

"Yes. At long last, Jesus will return for His people Israel and for His followers from among the Gentiles and bring an end to all unrighteousness. The Day of the Lord will be signaled by a great cosmic disturbance in the heavens when the sun and moon will grow dark, and the stars shall fall from the sky. Jesus had given a warning in Luke that those around when the Antichrist begins his persecution should flee to the mountains. Here, when Jesus returns, and these great signs signal His arrival in the heavens, and great earthquakes occur on the ground, it will be the enemies of the people of God that will flee to the mountains.

"Prior to His descent to the earth, He will send His angels to place the mark of God on the foreheads of 144,000 Jews who will remain on the earth as Jesus's witnesses, but will be protected from His wrath by the seal. The rest of the believers will be gathered from the four winds by His angels. Not only the living believers, but also and first, the dead in Christ, who will receive their resurrected bodies to live in the new kingdom of God. This is an event known as the Rapture. This is clearly the order in which the Bible teaches these events will occur: the treaty of death, the abomination that causes desolation and reveals the identity of the Antichrist, the Antichrist commences the Great Tribulation, Jesus returns at the Day of the Lord to deliver His people, He then purges the world of unrighteousness and defeats the Antichrist and his empire in the battle of Armageddon, the Kingdom of God is officially established, and the marriage supper of the Lamb to His Bride is held.

"Many people, though, conveniently the ones who do not wish to endure suffering and death, have a different theory that the church will be raptured before Daniel's seventieth week begins in what is known as the Pre-Tribulation Rapture. They mistakenly call the entire seventieth week of Daniel the 'tribulation period,' and there are those that even call the whole seventieth week the Day of the Lord. The Bible never once refers to the entire seventieth week as the 'tribulation period.' They believe in a pre-tribulation rapture based on the verse in Romans that says that we are not appointed to God's wrath. Paul was not in error to write this, but the mistake these people make is that they appoint the entire seventieth week to God's wrath. The Day of the Lord is, of course, the Day of God's wrath, but the persecution of the saints is not a part of God's wrath. It is man's wrath on the people of God.

"The Lord never promised us an escape from man's wrath. In fact, the opposite is true. Jesus promised us that His followers would suffer for His name's sake. We face man's wrath every day of our lives. I worry for people who believe such nonsense, as I don't believe they are preparing themselves to be the faithful people that Christ will look for when He returns. The apostles and early disciples of the church gave their lives for the name of Christ. They were willing to do this at any time, of course, but they especially lived out their martyr mentality in case they should be martyred in the final moments before Christ's return. As their successors, this is something that we all must be willing to embrace and something that we are all expected of as Christ's disciples."

CHAPTER 14

A year and six months had passed since LaMarcus had gotten saved. With all the time in the world to spend in the Bible, he and Mr. Curtis had gone through diligently every book of the Bible, and in some cases, more than once. LaMarcus had come a long way from when he had started walking with Jesus, but as every good Christian knows, life's not over until God calls you home, and until then, you have more room to grow and more the Lord wants to teach you.

On this day, however, when they were about to begin their study, the demeanor of Mr. Curtis seemed slightly off for some reason. Not by a whole lot, mind you, but his mind was definitely somewhere else. Every time LaMarcus would read something and wait for him to comment, his eyes would be staring out the window, or he'd be looking at LaMarcus with a blank look on his face.

"Hey," LaMarcus asked him. "Is everything all right?"

"Oh, yeah, everything's fine."

So LaMarcus kept reading, and Mr. Curtis kept staring off into space. LaMarcus was reading out of Psalms, and the plan for later in the day was to move on to Proverbs. Finally, Mr. Curtis began to react like his normal self and give out comments to the things LaMarcus was reading. It relieved LaMarcus a little bit, but he was curious as to why Mr. Curtis seemed so unresponsive beforehand.

After they had finished their morning study session, Mr. Curtis put his Bible back up and sat down on his bed, facing LaMarcus. "You know, when you think about it, you and I, we've been through quite a lot."

"Yeah, we have," LaMarcus agreed. "We haven't even known each other a full two years, but, hey, when ya got as much time as we have, two years feels like a lifetime."

Mr. Curtis chuckled a little. "Yep, I remember when you first came in here. You were a disrespectful, snot-nosed punk. And now look at you. You haven't even known the Lord that long, and already He's done amazing work in you. You have the heart of a disciple, LaMarcus. You're always eager to learn, and when you learn, you do it with devotion. You're a smart kid, and it's because you have put your mind into submission to the Lord in your studying and growth that God has replaced your ignorance with wisdom. I'll tell you what, as long as you continue to trust the Lord and let Him guide you, He is going to do a great work through you. There is no doubt in my mind."

LaMarcus felt humbled by everything he said. "Thanks. I remember when I first came here, everyone tried to spook me out, and for a minute, it worked. I thought you were a crazy old man. There was nothing about you that made any sense, and deep down, I really couldn't stand you, even though I put up with what I called your weirdness. But then you introduced me to Jesus, and my life changed forever. We used to be cellmates forced together, but now we're friends. In fact, I have to say that you are the best friend I have in this place and even the best friend I've ever had."

Mr. Curtis let out something of a sigh. "I'm proud of you, LaMarcus. I'm proud of the godly man you've become. Don't ever stop letting the Lord mold you even more into His design."

"Don't worry, Mr. Curtis," LaMarcus reassured him. "It's like we've talked about before. As long as we are still breathing, we can know that the Lord still wants to teach us something."

"Good. Don't ever lose that resolve," Mr. Curtis responded. "You have got such a fire within you, LaMarcus. I still have the same zeal, but I'm worn and don't have the same energy that I used to have. This is why it is important for the old to teach the young. If they don't know how to fight, how can they carry on? I have tried for years to get the young people to listen to me, but they did not have ears to hear. But the Lord gave you ears to hear, and you have gone through intense schooling that I like to call basic training. You have the spirit of a warrior, the eyes of a watchman, and I believe a tongue as sharp and cutting as a trumpet blast. This is a deadly combination when used for the will of Jesus. You have been greatly blessed, but now is the time to put these gifts to work in the real world as you have tried to do here with the other prisoners. As the citizens of Israel all are part of the military, so too are we all to be the soldiers of God's army.

"My prayer for you, LaMarcus, is that the fire never dies, but becomes as passionate as the prophet Jeremiah. I know you have a special place in your heart for the Jewish people. Always remember them in your prayers, and when you are sent to the places that God wants you to go, never exclude them from your conversations. Let everyone know that the land of Israel has not been forgotten or forsaken in the eyes of the Father. The nations will be judged for their treatment of Israel at the return of the King. Whenever you share the Gospel, do not neglect the kingdom of God. It is because of the coming kingdom that we must go forth with urgency. When the Lord returns, it will be too late for them to willingly give their lives to him. Such a fear is necessary to shake them to repentance. I know you know all of this, but it is good to be reminded."

"Don't worry about it. I understand," LaMarcus said. "It's going to be a long road, but, hey, God never said it would be easy. If I didn't have Jesus with me, I don't think I could do it. But I'm really lucky. I do have Jesus. He's all I need. And as a bonus, He's sent me you. Not only have you taught me what I know, but I know also that I'll have your support."

"Yes, you will have my support," Mr. Curtis said. "But understand that I didn't teach you anything. It is the Holy Spirit that teaches us, no matter where it is we learn." He then began to speak with a little concern. "You do understand that I won't always be there to hold your hand, right?"

"Yeah, I know," said LaMarcus. "I know we won't always be around each other, but I figure that we'll at least try to meet up on the outside, won't we?"

"It's hard to say, LaMarcus," said Mr. Curtis. "From the time that our respective releases come up, the Lord may lead us in different directions, and we may never see each other again until we get to heaven. I can't say what will happen one way or another. This is why I've been encouraging you to learn how to study on your own and have personal one-on-one time with the Spirit. I have done my best to answer your questions, but the Holy Spirit wants to teach you directly, and He will teach you better than I ever could. He will reveal things to you as you read the Word in the private hours with just you and him. Promise me that you will let the Lord personally teach you. Promise me so I know that when we're not together, you'll still put yourself in His hands and His guidance."

He said it with such urgency that it almost caught LaMarcus off guard. He looked Mr. Curtis dead in the eye and said, "I promise that no matter what, I will remain devoted to and under the instruction of God."

Mr. Curtis seemed satisfied with the answer. "I'm counting on you, LaMarcus. As I said earlier, you have to pick up where I left off. My body is broken to its core. By the grace of God, I have been like Paul and fought a good fight and ran a great race. As for me, I will continue to fight until the Lord takes me home, and I can finish my race. But the Lord's favor is now on you and your age. Do all things in the love and servitude of Christ and the Lord will honor your work."

"I most certainly will, Mr. Curtis," LaMarcus said.

Very casually and calmly Mr. Curtis reached out and put his hand on LaMarcus's shoulder. "You know I love you, kid. You're like a brother to me."

"I know, Mr. Curtis," LaMarcus said. "It's the same way over here. But we can wait 'til we leave this place to say goodbye. How 'bout we go stop by Mr. Patrick's office and read up on some Proverbs."

Mr. Curtis smiled and said, "Sure, LaMarcus. Sounds good."

When they got to Mr. Patrick's office, Mr. Patrick was in the middle of rearranging the furniture to accommodate for a new bookshelf he was putting in. He was so busy with what he was doing, he didn't even hear them come in.

"Is this a bad time?" Mr. Curtis asked him with a bit of sarcasm. "We can always come back."

Mr. Patrick looked up, a little startled. When he saw it was LaMarcus and Mr. Curtis, he settled down a little. "Oh, hey, you two. No, come on in. I could use a break." He opened up his Bible and began reading with them out of Proverbs. It was just like any of the previous meetings they had had over the last year and a half, which in case you're wondering occurred quite a lot, but not daily like the study time between LaMarcus and Mr. Curtis.

LaMarcus was completely oblivious to the heavy air that lingered from the demeanor of Mr. Curtis and also now Mr. Patrick. When it was LaMarcus's turn to read, he was unaware of the looks going back and forth between the two old men. If you would've been there, you would've seen a story being told in their eyes. It was like they were having their own conversation without speaking. They had been friends for a while, fifteen years in fact. Mr. Curtis first met Mr. Patrick back when he first joined the prison's staff. Mr. Curtis had already been there on a previous indictment for sharing Christ and welcomed a new friend with open arms and spent the rest of that year sharing testimonies before he was released.

Two years after his release, Mr. Curtis had been arrested again and was able to pick up his friendship with Mr. Patrick. Ever since, Mr. Curtis has remained in the exact same prison and in the exact same cell. Mr. Patrick had even been staffed long enough to be present during "the incident." These two certainly had a long history together.

When the group had finished with their reading of Proverbs and had their discussions afterwards, LaMarcus was feeling tired and was ready to head back to the cell.

"You go on ahead, LaMarcus," Mr. Curtis told him. "I'll be there in a little bit."

"All right. If I'm asleep then just let me be and we can pick up in the morning." With that, LaMarcus left the room and was escorted back to the cell by one of the two guards.

When LaMarcus was well away from the room, Mr. Patrick looked at Mr. Curtis and began to ask him, "Did you have a chance to tell him?"

"No," Mr. Curtis responded. "I tried to, but he wasn't picking up on my hints. He has absolutely no idea."

"I swear, sometimes you're too cryptic with your words. You should have been straight up with him," Mr. Patrick said.

"Maybe. Maybe I should have been this time. But honestly, would you expect me to be any different? It's always been part of my character to make people think," said Mr. Curtis.

"That it has, Luke. And I know you wouldn't have done it if you didn't think LaMarcus could handle it," said Mr. Patrick.

"Even still, I may do something else." Turning to his old friend, he quietly said, "Keep an eye on him for me, will ya? Don't let him do anything stupid."

"I'll treat him as my responsibility for as long as he's here," Mr. Patrick said.

"Thank you. I appreciate it." With that, he gave Mr. Patrick as big of a hug as he could with his hands still handcuffed and then headed out of the office back to his cell, the second guard in tow.

LaMarcus in the meantime, even as tired as he was, begun to wonder how long Mr. Curtis was going to stay over. He didn't have too much of a chance to really worry about it however as he began to doze off, and eventually the sleep just took over. Mr. Curtis returned to the cell and found his protégé knocked out on his bed. Mr. Curtis snickered at him and thought that it was probably for the best. He caught the attention of a nearby guard and asked for a piece of paper and pencil so that he could write a letter. When he had finished, he casually placed the letter in his Bible and placed the Bible back in its usual spot.

Several hours had passed by, well into the middle of the night, and LaMarcus was sound asleep. However, around the time that the night transitions from late night to early morning, LaMarcus began to dream a very disturbing dream. He was in the middle of an open field, much like being in the Sahara desert, but it was grassy and even a little rocky. Out in the middle of the field, LaMarcus saw a large herd of white sheep, who were all facing this one tiny little lamb who was speaking to them. LaMarcus couldn't tell what the lamb was saying, but it caused quite a commotion among the sheep. LaMarcus was at the top of a hill overlooking the scene, closer from where he had started. As he thought about getting closer, he missed the arrival of some more animal groups.

As the lamb was talking, from out of nowhere, a small pack of wolves being trailed by a pack of hyenas and a flock of vultures came through the field, making a beeline for the lamb. The sheep were too startled to consider stopping them, and the wolves quickly surrounded the little lamb. They circled around him and finally attacked him, each taking their own turns biting him. It was an unbearable sight for LaMarcus to behold. He could hardly take the cruelty of the wolves, as with each bite the lamb cried out in pain. When the lamb was covered in his own blood and his flesh seared, one of the wolves finished the job and took one final bite at the lamb's throat. The lamb gave out a terrible cry as it died, and then that same wolf grabbed it by the neck and tossed it into the view of the other sheep. Then the hyenas and vultures, being scavengers, attacked the dead body of the lamb and ripped it even more and even fought each other over whose turn it was to feast.

The wolves barked and broke up the commotion, and together with the hyenas and vultures began to mock the dead body of the little lamb. They threatened the other sheep with the same fate if any more of what the lamb had said was repeated. LaMarcus was shocked to see that some of the sheep suddenly turned into goats. These new goats encouraged the other sheep to do as they had done to avoid this outcome. The wolves moved in on those remaining sheep that would not turn to goats. The whole thing was too horrible to watch. Tears gushed down LaMarcus's face, and his anger surged as he witnessed the evil that these creatures portrayed.

Just when he finally made the determination to do something himself, he, and the wolves, were interrupted by a sudden, and extremely loud sound. It was so piercing and so frightening that it caused the feathers on the vultures to fly off, and the hyenas instantly cowered. The wolves tried to stand in place, but even they, too, became afraid. They frantically looked for the source of the sound. To LaMarcus, it sounded like a loud roar, like one from a lion. The sound of the roar dissipated and then picked back up again, only louder than before. LaMarcus realized why and so did the wolves. Standing about twenty feet to LaMarcus's right and about ten feet behind him, suddenly, was a giant lion. It had a crown on its head and stood in great majesty. It walked forward and stood parallel to LaMarcus and gave another roar.

After this roar was given, the wolves whimpered at the sight of something that appeared next to the lion. It was a little lamb, the same little lamb that the wolves had just viciously slain. He stood in the same style of glory as the lion, only a little less, and he had a long red streak on his back. LaMarcus looked harder and noticed that this red streak was blood, but it wasn't the same color blood that the lamb had spilled earlier. It was a different shade altogether. When he noticed this, LaMarcus just happened to catch out of the corner of his eye something on the lion he had not noticed before. On each of the lion's paws, there was a considerably large hole with dried blood stains, giving the indication that the lion's paws had been pierced by something. He also saw a long open wound on the side of the lion, again with dried blood stains. The color of the blood from the lion matched the color of the blood that was on the back of the lamb. LaMarcus concluded in his mind that this must indeed be the lion's blood.

The lion gave another quick roar, and all of the sheep who hadn't turned to goats were teleported up to the hill where the lion, lamb, and LaMarcus stood. Then the lion leaped down from the hill and devoured the wolves, all of which tried to fight back but were struck down by the ferocity of the lion. The lion then turned his attention to the hyenas and naked vultures and quickly dispensed of them. He then turned his attention to the goats. The goats were overcome with shame for their actions and pleaded for mercy from the lion. The lion did not show mercy, but instead of devouring them in his mouth, he took his paws and swiped them all down with his sharp claws. When he was finished, all of the sheep cheered at the victory of the lion, and LaMarcus himself even gave cheers for the lion.

After this, LaMarcus woke up at the sound of the morning meal bell. He looked over at the opposite bed and was surprised to see it already made, and Mr. Curtis was nowhere to be seen. "Oh well, he must already be at breakfast," LaMarcus thought. He couldn't wait to share this new dream with him and try to figure out what it might've meant.

As soon as he got to the prison mess hall, he kept looking but couldn't find Mr. Curtis anywhere. He got his food and went to their usual spot at the far end of the room. He wasn't there either. "Huh, well that's really strange," LaMarcus said out loud. It wasn't like Mr. Curtis to not be in their spot yet. LaMarcus continued to eat his breakfast and at no point did the old man ever show up.

LaMarcus returned to his cell and pulled out a book he had asked Mr. Patrick to borrow about a month back. It was a book that Mr. Curtis had recommended to him, written by a Chinese pastor named Watchman Nee, who lived back in the 1940s and died in a Chinese prison in the 1970s. Watchman Nee was very repetitive in his writings and often made very complex points that took LaMarcus quite a few readings of each section to get. For not being much of a reader, he found himself reading some of the hardest material he had ever encountered in his life.

Later during recreational time, LaMarcus sought after one of the guards to go ask Mr. Patrick if he had seen Mr. Curtis. The guard turned him down though, saying that Mr. Patrick wasn't in the prison today. LaMarcus was beginning to get worried now. He wondered if the Rapture had occurred, but he quickly struck that thought down, remembering what he had learned from Mr. Curtis.

Maybe he had a hearing he had to go to today, LaMarcus thought. *Even still, would a hearing take this long?*

The dinner call came and went, and still LaMarcus couldn't find Mr. Curtis. The night crept in, and by now, LaMarcus knew something was wrong. He began to become frantic and anxious. Finally, he stopped and just started praying. "Lord, I don't know where Mr. Curtis is, but you do. Help me to stop being anxious and trust that you have him well in your hands. Please, Lord, don't leave me hanging on what's going on for too long. I don't know how much more I can take." Not long after he finished his prayer, LaMarcus fell asleep as if being covered by a veil.

LaMarcus slept in, missing the morning meal, but was delivered a tray of food that was sitting at his door for a good hour. LaMarcus had no choice. He had to eat something, so he devoured the cold eggs, grits, toast, and warm juice sitting on his tray. Still, there was no sign that Mr. Curtis had ever returned the night before, as his bed was still made up the same way. Trying to get his mind off of it, he turned on the radio to one of the local Christian music stations. He then began to just stare out the window and soak in the sunlight that shined through.

Suddenly, he heard a noise behind him. He quickly turned around and looked in the direction of the cell door and saw Mr. Patrick standing there with a guard. LaMarcus could barely contain his excitement. "Mr. Patrick!" he said, rushing to the cell door. "What's going on? Where's Mr. Curtis?"

Mr. Patrick looked at the guard who took his keys and began to open the cell door. He then said, "Could you give us a minute?" The guard looked at him suspiciously. "Don't worry, I'm not taking him anywhere." The guard walked out of the cell and stood against the wall in between LaMarcus's cell and the one next door.

CHAPTER 15

Turning to LaMarcus, Mr. Patrick continued with the gravest voice LaMarcus had ever heard him use. "LaMarcus, you may want to sit down."

"Mr. Patrick, just tell me, where is he? Where's Mr. Curtis?" LaMarcus said, letting his emotions get the best of him.

"He's not here anymore, LaMarcus. He went home."

"He got released? I don't believe it. That's great. I'm happy for him," LaMarcus said.

"No, LaMarcus, he didn't get released," said Mr. Patrick. LaMarcus's face went from a face of joy to a face of shock. "LaMarcus, he's gone. He's dead."

If glass existed in the human brain, LaMarcus's would've cracked and then shattered. His face turned pale, and he felt like he was going to throw up. "Dead?" he questioned. "What do you mean, he's dead?"

Mr. Patrick swallowed as a grimaced look appeared on his face. "He was executed just last night."

LaMarcus's heart almost stopped beating. "Executed? He was executed?!"

"Yes, he was. Two days ago, after you came to my office, he was grabbed by the guards and taken to solitary confinement. The next morning he was taken to the courthouse and was displayed in front of a judge for a mock trial. Lawyers reamed him, claiming the same accusations that had been thrown at him his entire life. They spent four hours putting him down. They gave him little chance to defend himself.

Any time he spoke, he tried once again to share the Gospel with them. They used this as a chance to belittle him even more.

"After his trial, they took him to a cage set up on a Mardi Gras float. The whole city was set up like a parade. As the float roamed the city, people tossed their beads and moon pies and all else while the crowds would point and laugh at him and make fun of him. After humiliating him in the parade, they took him to Bienville square and tied him to a post. The crowds took their time, each taking a turn at getting a good hit on him. Then the crowds spent time throwing eggs at him. Then someone shouted that the eggs needed to be cooked, so they grabbed a hot iron and seared his feet. He was left there for some time as a spectacle for the people who would walk by.

"By nighttime, the main crowds came back and carried him back to the courthouse. They had torches set up in a circle at the front of the courthouse with a mass crowd gathered. He was placed in the middle of the area that the torches surrounded and brought to his knees. Everyone in the crowd was wearing masks like you'd see at a Mardi Gras ball, and finally, a man appeared in a jester style outfit with a more Italian style hat, complete with a feather. He also wore a mask and had a long, very real sword attached to his belt. He drew the sword and walked in circles around Mr. Curtis. The crowd roared as he pumped them up. Mr. Curtis, never giving up, began to pray out loud, only to draw more spite from the crowd. He prayed the same way as Stephen in Acts: that God would not hold what they did against them. The man with the sword had enough and kicked him hard in the back, much to the crowd's delight. He then used his foot to nudge Mr. Curtis forward in a leaning position. The crowd became silent, and then the executioner lined himself up, screamed, and brought his sword to the back of his neck. The blade was dull, and multiple swings were taken to sever his head. The Lord showed mercy on Mr. Curtis, however. He was gone after the first swing and never had to feel the repeated hacks. The crowd erupted in cheers, and the executioner took off his glove, dipped his hands in Mr. Curtis's blood, and proceeded to lick his fingers. The whole thing was purely satanic."

Obviously, by this point, LaMarcus was bursting in tears. "Why would any of them care about if he died?"

"Did he never tell you why he was arrested?" Mr. Patrick asked.

"He did. He said every time he was arrested it was for preaching the Gospel, no matter where he went," LaMarcus said.

"Everywhere he went. Mr. Curtis was from here, yes, but he travelled throughout the nation. He had written books and knew some people who let him guest speak in their churches and on their radio shows. He was nationally known, and he was turning heads with his heavy, convicting messages. Finally, the enemies he made, which were plenty from every community, made moves to get laws passed against him and others like him. When he still wouldn't stop proclaiming what God told him, they rigged the system to put him in prison indefinitely until they could legally find a way to execute him. They wanted to make him an example."

LaMarcus was already on the floor by this point, but the more Mr. Patrick talked of their treatment of Mr. Curtis, the more it made LaMarcus sick to his stomach. Finally, he couldn't take it anymore, and he rushed over to the toilet and threw up. Mr. Patrick's face grimaced at the sight of it. It was not because of LaMarcus throwing up. It was because of the reason why he was. When LaMarcus was done, he plopped back on the floor like a dead fish and laid there in misery.

"I'm sorry to be the one to tell you, LaMarcus. I know how much he meant to you. He meant a lot to me too. He was a great friend. I'll be right back with some water for your mouth." With that, Mr. Patrick left the cell, and about ten minutes later, he came back with two large cups of water; one to help remove the taste of vomit from LaMarcus's mouth and the other just for him to drink and get some life back.

Several hours after Mr. Patrick gave him the water and left the cell again, LaMarcus was left to cope with the new reality that was set upon him. His mind was adrift, reliving the rocky start the two had had when he arrived, when Mr. Curtis had taken the time to warn him of his impending doom but also of the salvation from that doom paid for by Jesus. He remembered the countless hours of training and studying the Word. He remembered the hours upon hours of prayer that they had prayed. They prayed for the nation, they prayed for Israel, they prayed for Christians around the world.

They spent hours listening to Christian radio talk programs. LaMarcus had learned a lot from these radio shows that he could apply to his own personal study. His favorites were the show with the funny talking Scottish man preaching to his congregation, and on the weekends, the intellectual Christian apologist who emphatically spoke against atheism.

Also on the radio, they had listened to Christian music. Mr. Curtis had shared with him his favorites, and LaMarcus began to develop his own favorites different than that from Mr. Curtis. Both of LaMarcus's favorites were obviously in the Christian rap genre. One was the guy who rapped about going to church in street clothes in one song and in another about how people talk in circles but in the end aren't talking about anything. His other favorite was that really popular white rapper, who Mr. Curtis thought was overrated.

LaMarcus did still like some of the artists and styles that Mr. Curtis liked. Mr. Curtis even taught him a bunch of songs that used to come on the radio but don't anymore, because radio of any genre is now the same ten songs over and over, and maybe in the late hours you'll hear some old stuff.

There were a lot of good memories in that prison cell for LaMarcus. In fact, they were the best memories that he had to share with people. LaMarcus wasn't proud of his old life, so why share it, except to warn others of what he went through and what brought him out of it?

Then LaMarcus began to think about the last day he saw Mr. Curtis alive. Mr. Curtis's words seemed to replay over and over like a broken record. Then, all of a sudden, a light bulb clicked on in LaMarcus's head. *He knew*, LaMarcus said to himself. *He knew what was about to happen. He knew he was fixing to die. And he was trying to tell me, but I wouldn't listen. Ugh, I am such an idiot!* LaMarcus was now angry at himself, and he realized, if he had picked up on what Mr. Curtis was telling him, he would've had a chance to say goodbye. That made LaMarcus really sink into a cloud of depression.

Over the next week, LaMarcus hardly ever came out of his cell. He just spent his time curled up and sulking. He barely ate the meals the guards brought him when he wouldn't show up at meal times. Worst of all, he wasn't reading the Bible. He let emotion take over and run his life. And he started to become bitter at God for taking away his mentor.

After that first week had passed and LaMarcus was still sulking in his cell, suddenly, new thoughts entered his mind, and they hit him hard. They were passages of Scripture that were being thrown at him like baseballs. One was when Moses was first being assigned the task of leading the Hebrews out of the land of Egypt. With every excuse Moses came up with, the Lord had an answer, until finally, the Lord became angry and said, "Who made man's mouth? Or the dumb or deaf or the seeing or the blind? Did not I, the Lord?" Now in Exodus, Moses still continued to defy what God was telling him by asking the Lord to send another with him to speak, and the Lord became angrier with him, because Moses feared the people more than the very God of his forefathers that was standing right before him. But the words which God had spoken prior are what stuck with LaMarcus.

Then his mind flashed to Job. Job, in the midst of his trials, never once renounced his faith in the one true God. However, that didn't mean he didn't have questions for God. Near the end of the book, Job begins to break down and ask, in paraphrasing, "Why, oh God, why?" In God's long rebuttal to Job, he opens with a very simple question: "Where were you when I laid the foundations of the earth?"

LaMarcus began to realize that God was talking to him at that moment. LaMarcus had been questioning God's decisions and was shaking his fist at Him. He was not trusting that the Lord knew what He was doing and that He had a plan in all of this. Then another verse popped in his head, one that he had read on the last day he saw Mr. Curtis. "Trust in the Lord with all your heart," the book of Proverbs tells us, "And lean not on your own understanding, but in all ways acknowledge Him and He will direct thy path."

LaMarcus was humbled by this conversation with the Lord, and he repented of his lack of faithfulness. It was time to let the Lord teach him directly as Mr. Curtis had stressed he needed to do. LaMarcus then went over to Mr. Curtis's old bed and pulled out the Bible to read it. He noticed a giant space between the pages and pulled out a sheet of paper. It was the letter that Mr. Curtis had written the night he was taken away. LaMarcus opened it up and began to read.

LaMarcus,

I'm sure, if you're reading this, that by now I'm probably dead. It's been coming for a while now. These poor people think that they'll be solving a problem by killing me, when I'm but one in a sea of faces of people just like me. The work of Jesus, even in the darkest hours of the Antichrist's reign, will continue on, and will not stop just because they think it should. I don't know, nor will I predict, that you will end up like me and be given a martyr's death. If you are, I pray that you will embrace it with humility and servitude just like I am disciplining myself to do, even now as I write.

Life is going to be harder for you, kid. Even though I suffered various things, I still lived most of my life in a country that understood freedom. You, however, do not have that luxury. Where I was given a massive platform, your platform may be one street corner. I would advise, in anything the Lord leads you to do, that you find and partner yourself with the underground church. You will need each other in the coming future.

Ultimately, the Lord is going to have to lead you to where He wants you to go. Only He knows your destiny and it is not your job to figure out what it is, but to listen for what the Lord is telling you it is. If you want my advice, I would pray earnestly during the rest of your time in prison, and if you are not hearing any direction from the Lord, then don't make up the Lord's mind.

If you don't hear any direction, I advise you to stay here in the city and look for something the Lord may want you to do here first. A good place to start would be on the streets. You have been where they are. You know how they think. They are throwing their lives away. But now, not only does God have an agent with His message, but one who can relate to them better than most pastors today could. Point is, in the Lord, you always look for opportunity, but you don't ever create opportunity. That's not your job to do. It's like I've told you a thousand times. Don't get ahead of God.

As for me, kid, you don't need to worry about and fret about me or anything I'm fixing to go through. Whatever they got in store for *me, I'll take on with joy like James and Paul said we should do. It really is the least I can do after all that Christ did for me. How can I call myself a Christian if I'm not willing to lay my life down, even unto death the same way that my King did for me? It doesn't make me a good servant or a good friend, does it? It ain't that bad, and it's nothing compared to eternity anyway, so it's worth it.*

As I told you, you're going to have your own share of sufferings and persecution, but don't let it distress you, kid. You have access to the power of God, the same power that raised His Son from the dead. Let Jesus use that power in you, and you will be a worthy witness to this broken world. And speaking of witnesses, not only do you have Jesus working in you, with you, and for you, as if you needed anything else, you also have your own cheering section. Remember in Hebrews 12 when it talks about how we are surrounded by a great cloud of witnesses. All the saints of old, cheering us on as we run our race and praying for us when we stumble, because we are all family and one in Christ. And you can bet your life that when I join that group, I'll be cheering extra hard for you.

Well, kid, it's about time for me to go. It's been a privilege to get to know you and disciple you. Like I told you before, I'm proud of you, and I can't wait to see the work that God is going to do through you. From one brother in Christ to another, I love you, LaMarcus.

Your friend,
Mr. Curtis

CHAPTER 16

LaMarcus woke up with the sun shining through his window brighter than it had shined in a while. He made up his bed, put on his shoes, and went down to the mess hall for one last morning meal. The crowd of inmates in the mess hall had mixed reactions to seeing him. Over the last few years, he had done his best to share Jesus with each of them, but to no avail. Shortly after Mr. Curtis's death, his world, at least from the outside, had spiraled downward. Anytime LaMarcus shared his faith, he was mocked and occasionally beat. LaMarcus never fought back like he used to before he was saved.

Even though none of them took him up on his offer to learn about Christ, some of the inmates did eventually start to show respect to LaMarcus, because he had been diligent in his sharing. They didn't agree with him or think they needed Jesus, but they respected his devotion and the way he lived out what he believed. It was more than they had seen from some of these other "Christians" back home.

Once, a Muslim inmate had gotten into a huge debate with LaMarcus over Islam versus Christianity. The Muslim didn't leave convicted about the things LaMarcus was saying—in fact, he was enraged and tried to kill LaMarcus later, which resulted in him being sent to a maximum security prison—but LaMarcus simply let the Muslim inmate talk about what Islam was, pointed out where he lied about what a Muslim believes, thanks to his training with Mr. Curtis, and compared it with Christianity. He didn't argue theology, he simply stated facts: this is what you believe, this is what I believe. Then he looked at the crowd of inmates and said,

"Clearly Allah, the god of the Quran, and Yahweh, the God of the Bible, are not the same. So if you ever decided that you wanted to follow a god, which of the two seems more appealing? Who would be the better one to follow?" The crowd overwhelmingly said Yahweh, but most followed up with, "But I'm not going to convert or anything." What LaMarcus never learned was that some of these inmates would be confronted with this same issue again and, remembering his words, actually choose to follow Jesus.

On this day, however, nothing could wreck LaMarcus's spirit. In a few short hours, he would begin the process of being released from prison. He had spent five total years in this prison and was now being let out on good behavior. Everything seemed to be better on this day. The morning meal didn't taste as bad. The whole of the prison didn't smell as bad. The anticipation LaMarcus felt was immense. Freedom for the first time in five years: it seemed like an idea that you had to see to believe. Of course, he had found freedom a few years prior, but now, in his freedom from a physical prison, he was ready to share the spiritual freedom he had received to the city, country, world, and even other planets if possible.

The hours between the morning meal and the release process were some of the longest hours LaMarcus had ever experienced. He spent most of them in the Bible, Psalms specifically, and as he read, he rejoiced right along with King David or whichever other psalmist he read from. All in all, he could've spent his time studying the maps, and it wouldn't have made any difference. He was like a kid on the last day of school or any adult who quits a job they don't like.

Finally, around midday, a guard came to get him, saying all was in order. LaMarcus grabbed the Bible and the radio and was escorted by the guard to a different area of the prison. The warden and captain were waiting at a desk, going through all the legal paperwork that they needed to do. They told LaMarcus where to sign, legally consenting to the release. After this, the same guard from before led him to a bathroom with a sink in it. He took possession of the Bible and radio and handed LaMarcus a box with his clothes in it. LaMarcus changed his clothes and noticed there was a razor and shaving cream on the sink for him to use, so he shaved off what little hair he had grown.

When he was finished, the guard handed him back the Bible and radio, re-cuffed him, and proceeded to the final phase of the process. Here, LaMarcus received back everything he had in his possession at the time of his arrest, with the exception of the .45 pistol that was tucked in his pants. This, of course, was a part of evidence. After signing a form stating the return of this property, LaMarcus was escorted outside the prison, un-cuffed, and was told by the guard, "You're free to go."

Mr. Patrick was outside waiting for him. He had promised to give LaMarcus a ride home, something LaMarcus was grateful for. Even with the prison in the city, it was still a good walk to his hood. Once they got to the general area, LaMarcus had him pull over.

"I can go ahead and walk the rest of the way. Mama doesn't know I'm coming. I'm gonna surprise her."

After Mr. Patrick pulled over, the two of them said their goodbyes and LaMarcus walked home. He took his time. He looked all around, soaking it all in. He hadn't seen his hood in five years, but now, here he was. Seeing it again, he thought to himself, *The prison looked like a palace compared to this dump*. Still, his dump was like a palace compared to other places around the world.

After walking a couple blocks, he turned around one corner and there it was, a baby blue house with the fanciest mailbox on the block. A friend of his Mama's had painted the mailbox to look like a fancy house in its own right. He looked at the front yard, and the same weeds that were growing by the door when he left were still there. He looked in the driveway, and he saw his Mama's old beat up Toyota Camry sitting in the same spot. He looked at the roof of the house, and there in the right front corner of the house was the same section of damage he had caused when he lit bottle rockets in the front yard and received the whippin' of his life from his Mama.

Without walking to the backyard, LaMarcus could still see his Mama's flower garden, and up next to the side of the house in the driveway, were three bikes: one was his, one was Jacoby's, and one was KayShawn's old bike. There was no doubt about it. LaMarcus was home. A new-found appreciation surged through LaMarcus as he walked up to the front door. Not knowing if it was locked or not, he went ahead and knocked on it. He could hear a woman screaming from the other side of the door.

"Jacoby is not here. That boy may be running around doing God knows what, but you are not bringing that gang business to my house anymore!"

"Ma!" he shouted back. "Open up. It's me."

The door began to open, and there stood his mother, curlers and slippers alike, looking on with a look of surprise on her face. "LaMarcus? Is that you?" she asked.

"Yes, ma'am. It's me. I'm back."

Her face turned to sheer joy as she began to reach out her arms. "LaMarcus. LaMarcus, my baby!" She reached out and hugged him tight. "Oh-ho-ho, my baby boy has come home. Goodness, look at you. You've grown up so much. When did you get out?"

"Just today, Mama. I didn't call because I wanted to surprise you."

"Well, you certainly did." Before continuing, she stopped herself, and her voice changed to that motherly stern tone. "Now, LaMarcus, you're not going to go back to all of those silly ways that you did that got you arrested now, are you?"

LaMarcus felt embarrassed. "No, Mama, I'm not doing those things no more. I'll still hang out with the boys, but my gang days are over."

His mother let out a sigh that was half relief and half unsure. "Well, your friends are nice kids when they're not running around, stirring up trouble. At least you're getting out. Maybe while you're here, you can get your brother out too. I don't like his attitude one bit, LaMarcus. Ever since you left, he hasn't been the same. He hasn't been involved as much as you and KayShawn were, but that child of mine has come close to getting in trouble one too many times, and by God, I ain't gonna stand for it no more. Now I want you to go and talk some sense into him. Else, I'll make that boy understand with my old friend, Mr. Skillet."

LaMarcus chuckled at the idea of his brother being beaten by his mother with a skillet in her hand. "I will, Mama, but first, let me tell you why I'm not gonna do the gang no more. It's because while I was in prison, I got right with God, and now I follow Jesus."

"I already know, baby," she told him. "Thomas and Kelvin came by after they were released. They told me about what you did and how you changed. They seemed pretty disgusted by it, but it made me really think. And the more I thought about it, I decided to start going to church again. While I was there, I felt the Lord convict me, LaMarcus. I raised three children without Him, and I did all three of you wrong. I realized how much I needed Him, and so I let Jesus into my heart too."

LaMarcus was overjoyed to hear his mother tell him this. "That's great, Mama. God answered my prayer with you. Jacoby, I don't know where his head is, but we're going to keep praying for him. Where is he, Mama?"

"Baby, he's down by the court with everyone else," she answered.

"All right. I'm gonna head down there. See you when I get back, all right?" LaMarcus said.

"Okay, baby. You be careful. I just got you back. I don't want to lose you again."

With that, LaMarcus began to head for the basketball court, which was about halfway between his house and where the school was. As he approached it, there, for the first time in five years, he saw his little brother. Kelvin and Thomas were there, too, along with Thomas's girl, Drea. He didn't see anyone else there, but it didn't matter that much. He was here for his brother. Jacoby was on the court, dribbling the basketball. He pretended he was doing some juke moves on a defender and then ran the ball in for a layup. LaMarcus couldn't wait any longer.

"Jacoby! How many times have I told you about planting that foot down on that layup, bruh?"

Jacoby turned around when he heard the voice, and when he saw his brother standing there, he got a big smile on his face and ran toward him. "Yo, LaMarcus!" When he got to LaMarcus, he high-fived him and gave him a brotherly hug. "Dawg, I can't believe it. You're out!"

"That's right, baby, I'm home." They walked back to the others, who all took their turns welcoming back their comrade.

"So man, you ready to get back in the game?" Kelvin asked.

"The game?" LaMarcus asked. "I thought y'all were getting out of it."

"Well, we are. It's just that every now and then we need a little bit of extra cash, and when that happens, we got to do what we got to do," Kelvin said.

"Then you're not really giving it up," LaMarcus said. "All that talk back in prison, and in the end, you still can't let it go?"

"What are you saying, LaMarcus?" Jacoby asked. "Are you saying you ain't in the crew no more?"

"Y'all will always be my boys, but no, I can't do all those things I used to do. That's the old me. I'm a different person now," LaMarcus said.

Thomas rolled his eyes. "Oh, yeah, that's right. You went and got all religious on us. Now you're all better than us, right, cause you found God."

"No, Thomas, I'm not better than you," LaMarcus said. "I'm still just as human as any one of y'all. The only difference is that I've decided to live my life for Jesus Christ."

Turning to Jacoby, Kelvin's eyes got wide as he pointed at LaMarcus. "See, it's like we told you."

Jacoby looked at LaMarcus, not believing what he was hearing. "Wait, wait, wait. You really are a religious freak now? You, of all people, are religious?"

"Naw, I ain't religious," LaMarcus said.

"Dawg, you sittin' here talking 'bout Jesus and all of that. How are you not religious?" Kelvin shouted.

"I told you before, man. Religion is a list of rules you follow because you have to obey Him. I don't feel like I have to just obey Him. I want to obey Him. I want to follow Him. I'm able to know Him on a personal level that religion won't let you get to. I have a relationship with God the Father through His Son, Jesus Christ."

"I can't believe you're still preaching this same ridiculous crap," Thomas said.

"Y'all are the ones who brought it up. I was going to leave it alone," LaMarcus argued.

"Geez, bruh, I've heard of prison changing people, but this is crazy," Jacoby said.

"You're one to talk about changes, little g," LaMarcus said to him. "What's all this junk I hear about you running around in my old life? You never once cared for how we rolled before I was arrested, now all of a sudden you walk around like you're all bad. What are you trying to prove? That you're worthy of being my brother or KayShawn's brother? You're worthy to be my brother for no other reason than you're my brother. You don't have to throw your life away like I did or like KayShawn did."

"You were gone, LaMarcus," Jacoby fired back. "I didn't know what I was supposed to do."

"Well, I'm here now. So the question is, what are you going to do now?" He looked over at Thomas and Kelvin. "What are you two going to do now? Come on you guys. Whether you follow God or not, that's your choice, but you all know where this road leads. You stay involved in this life, and it only leads to iron bars or death. This life is filled with depression, misery, rage, and regret. Truth is, that's where any life apart from Christ will get ya. But look at our families. Look at our lives so far. They're broken for many reasons, but among the top is because we've been pouring into them these kinds of things. Rich people, their lives are broken too. They have all this money, and they think it gives them security. We have our crime spree, spreading fear so that it will give us security. Neither us nor the rich people have any security at all. There's only one person who can give us security. Only one person who can make our lives mean something. That person is Jesus."

"LaMarcus, let's say you're right. Let's say Jesus is the answer we need," Kelvin said. "What would he want with a bunch of criminals like us? Why would he ever look our way and care about us?"

"Simply put, Kelvin, He loves His creations. Too often we think we have to win God's approval, but He loved us even though we're sinners. Why would He love sinners? The idea is beyond human understanding but it's part of the awesomeness of God. If He didn't love sinners, then none of us would have any hope."

Now, while LaMarcus was talking, there was a group of about eight black guys heading toward the court. The one in the middle was the leader, and he didn't have an ounce of fat on him. Once they had gotten on the court, the leader yelled out, "Hey! What are y'all doing on my court?"

LaMarcus and the others were startled, and as they turned around, they saw who it was, and they formed a line. The new group of guys were from a rival hood, and here on the court, LaMarcus and company were outnumbered two to one.

"This ain't your court, Tank!" Thomas yelled at him. "Y'all have your own court on your side, so why don't you crawl back over there!"

Tank didn't take the callous look off his face. "Yeah, maybe I got my own court, but maybe I want this one too."

"Yeah! Why don't you come and take it then!" Thomas yelled. The rival group started to walk forward, but stopped when LaMarcus interjected.

"Shut up, Thomas!" he yelled. Tank looked over LaMarcus, trying to recognize him.

"Hey, wait a minute. I know you. You're KayShawn's brother. Well, I'm glad to see you're out, cause I remember that mark you left on my turf, and now I think I'll pay you back." The mark that Tank was talking about was the symbol of LaMarcus's gang that LaMarcus had graffitied on the side of Tank's house.

LaMarcus took a couple of steps forward. "Listen, I know we have our history. We both did each other wrong. Let's not do this anymore."

Tank was surprised to hear this kind of talk come from LaMarcus. "Would y'all get a load of this? When did you become such a softie? Well, you're wrong, boy, cause I'm gonna take it out of you right now." Tank then punched LaMarcus in the gut and just as swiftly gave him a right hook across the face.

"LaMarcus!" Jacoby yelled as he readied to rush in and help.

"All of you stay back!" LaMarcus yelled. He got up and locked his eyes on Tank. "This isn't going to solve anything, man. You can take out your anger on me and then them, but who's next, Tank? Will that anger ever subside?"

"Well, we'll just have to wait and see." Tank attacked him again, and LaMarcus went down again. Tank was in disbelief about the whole thing. "What the heck is this? You're not even going to fight back? What happened to you? What would your brother say if he saw this right now?

You know what he'd say. I know what he'd say. He would say that you're not a real brother. That's what I would think he would say."[3]

"I don't live to make a ghost proud anymore, Tank. I live for someone much better than you and I could ever hope to be," LaMarcus said.

"Well, that's a pretty tall order, but give me a name and I'll knock him down a couple pegs," Tank said sadistically.

"He's right here. I'd love to see you try," LaMarcus replied.

"Where? One of them?" Tank asked, confused.

"No, not them. It's someone you've been running from your whole life. You built your empire to show Him that you don't need Him. You've stood in defiance of Him your whole life. But it's never enough, is it? The more you build the empire, the more unhappy you remain, so you look for more to add to it. Look at you, Tank. You're the baddest of the bad. You got the money, the cars, the guns, the women, the rep. You have everything. Everybody knows you and locks their doors when you come near. You should be happy, but we both know better, don't we? You have everything you think you need, but you still feel empty. You still feel miserable, and because you can't figure out why, you feel angry and in pain."

"Oh yeah, Mr. Fortuneteller, how do you figure all of that about me?" Tank said.

"It's simple. My friend told me, and He's right. I can see it all over your face. You know what I'm saying is true," LaMarcus said.

"Very well, who is this magic, invisible friend, huh?" Tank asked. "Who is it that I, Tank, have been running from then, punk?"

"You really want to know? I think you know already. My friend, the one you've been running from, is Jesus Christ," LaMarcus said.

Tank didn't know how to react to what LaMarcus was telling him. "Jesus? You're friends with Jesus? So that's it, that's all you got? You think I need Jesus in my life?"

"I know you need Jesus in your life. We all do," LaMarcus answered.

Tank shook his head. "I don't need nobody telling me how to live my life. I don't care about getting right with no God, okay? In fact,

---

3   Worldly fictional characters may use stronger expletives in real life, but as a believer, I've followed biblical principles by not using coarse language.

there's only one god in these streets, all right, and that's me. I am the only god in these streets."

LaMarcus walked up to him, nose to nose, and defiantly said, "Not anymore. The God of gods is taking back what is rightfully His."

Tank was startled by LaMarcus's boldness. He then began to snicker as he backed up. "Okay. Okay. Fine then, Mr. Preacher man." He then quickly drew out his gun. "Jesus has saved you, right? Let's see if he can save you from this." He pressed the trigger, but the gun jammed. He cocked it and fired again at LaMarcus, but this time, the gun kicked back like it was on empty. Tank took out the magazine and saw it was still full of bullets. He checked the gun itself and sure enough, there was one shot in the chamber. He freaked out and demanded one of his buddies give him their gun. He fired at LaMarcus, but once again, there was a jam. This continued until all of the guns from Tank's crew were jammed. Tank was overcome with panic. He dropped the gun he was holding and stood before LaMarcus, trembling.

LaMarcus looked at the gun and then looked at Tank. "The Lord has spared my life today, and if you will listen, He wants to spare yours as well. Humans are a fallen creature, Tank. We are sinners. We turned away from God, our very Creator, and the just punishment is death. We are all promised an eternal death in hell. We'll cry out to God to have mercy, but He won't hear us. It will be too late. A day is coming, a day in which the Lord God Almighty will seek vengeance upon all the unrighteous. It will be a time of great wrath and no one will be able to bear it.

"But God, in this very hour, is gracious and merciful and so loving that He is giving us a second chance. Our sin condemns us, but there is a way that we can be set free from its curse. Jesus put Himself on a cross, bearing all of our sin on Himself, and by the shedding of His blood, He paid the penalty for our sin, if we choose to believe in him. And that's just the beginning. After three days, the power of the Father raised His Son from the dead, and if we believe in Jesus, we are not only reconciled to Him in this life, but also in eternity. We have life abundant on Earth and everlasting life for eternity, because Jesus is alive, but it is only available to those who believe. Jesus is coming back again. After the day of His wrath, He will set up a kingdom on Earth. And all those who believe in Him shall share in its inheritance.

"You're doing all of this on your own, but it is doomed to fail. Christ can change you into a person you never thought you'd be. He is strong where you are weak. You are living a broken life, but God wants to fix you into something for His grand design. Think about your life. That void you have in all of your possessions. That void is for him. Can't you see you need him?"

At that point, Tank felt conviction from the Holy Spirit. He fell on his knees before LaMarcus, and cried. LaMarcus got down on the ground with him and put his hand on his shoulder. Tank began the most awkward informal prayer you have ever heard, but it was from his heart. The man who was once the most well-known gang leader in the city, died that day, and out of the ashes, a new creation led by Jesus was born.

As both crews watched the scene unfold, they were shocked at what they were witnessing. Thomas, especially, could not believe his eyes. "What just happened?" he asked.

"He just made one of the toughest men in town cry by sharing about God," Jacoby said. The whole thing moved on the hearts of Thomas, Kelvin, and Jacoby. They began to listen now to what LaMarcus had to say, for they witnessed with their own eyes the power of the Living God. In short order, the very trio who had rejected LaMarcus's transformation were transformed, themselves.

LaMarcus began holding Bible studies at his house, and he shared with them all that he had learned in prison. The attitude of the whole community changed. With the breakdown of gang violence, everyone felt safer and more unified together. Tank himself, who five years prior would've been shot by LaMarcus for entering his house, was attending and even leading the Bible studies at LaMarcus's house. The two men led the charge in replacing gang violence in the city with Jesus Christ. It was quite the turnaround and quite the revival that many Christians in the city had long been praying for. God was moving in the poor communities of the city, but LaMarcus knew that it was only a matter of time that the Spirit of God would once again come to blows with the pride of the richer communities.

CHAPTER 17

I t didn't take too long after Tank became a believer for the media to pick up on what was happening in LaMarcus's hood. Rumors about the most notorious gang leader of the city suddenly turning to Jesus spread through the heart of downtown Mobile like wildfire. The local news stations rushed to find out the truth. Their attention had been drawn by Tank's conversion, but Tank pointed them in the direction of LaMarcus, saying "God sent this man right here, an ex-con in his own right, to show me how God really loves me. Of the two of us, he is the one you need to talk to. If you ask me, I think he specifically has been chosen by God."

At first, the reporters didn't seem to buy it, but when Tank insisted further, they finally began asking LaMarcus questions as well. LaMarcus was captivating. The wisdom that God gave him to answer their questions left the reporters speechless. Almost weekly, new reports would come out of the change to the neighborhood and how its effects spread to others, as crimes related to gang activities shrank to its lowest in the previous fifteen years. Many within the city, especially the leaders and the hundreds that showed up on the day of Mr. Curtis's execution, could not believe the growing spark of the new "Christ movement." It was a major setback for them. They had just made a spectacle of the death of a well-known Christian, and now suddenly Christianity was growing in the streets. How was this possible?

As LaMarcus was driving one day with Mr. Patrick, he thought about the transformation that had occurred, and if he had told this story to anyone ten years ago, they'd have laughed him out of town. Now they were driving in a part of town that LaMarcus had been to maybe once in his life before, and this was only a middle class area. They pulled into the church parking lot, and LaMarcus was getting nervous. In his head, he started praying that God would work this out. He and Mr. Patrick walked around to where the church offices were located. Just inside the doors sat a desk where a young woman secretary was typing.

She spotted the two of them almost immediately and asked, "Can I help you, gentlemen?"

LaMarcus was the one to speak up. "Yes, we were wondering if the pastor was in right now. We would like to have a meeting with him."

"I'm sorry," she said, "he's in, but he's extremely busy today. Generally, we schedule the meetings in advance, so..." She didn't get to finish, because another voice interrupted her.

"It's okay, Stacy," the voice said. LaMarcus and Mr. Patrick turned to see a man about in his midthirties, standing there. "My meeting I was supposed to have in a few minutes just called and cancelled. Maybe it's because I was supposed to meet with them instead."

"Yes, sir," she responded.

Turning his attention to the two strangers before him, the young pastor said, "Gentlemen, how are you today?"

"Doing well, sir. Doing well. How are you?" asked Mr. Patrick.

"I'm fine as well. I'm Keith Mills. I'm the senior pastor here," he said.

"I'm Joe Patrick, and this is my friend," Mr. Patrick said, reaching for LaMarcus.

"Hello, sir, I'm LaMarcus Russell."

The pastor's eyes seemed to shift as if he recognized the name. "LaMarcus Russell?" he pondered. "Are you the young kid that's leading the movement downtown?"

"Yes, sir. That's me," LaMarcus answered.

"Well, I'm pleased to have you here. I've read all about what's been happening, and I'm so proud to see growing leaders in the up and coming generations. The Lord is really blessing your work," Pastor Mills said.

"Thank you, sir," LaMarcus said. "And that's actually the reason that I am here."

"I'm not sure I understand," said Pastor Mills.

"As you said, God's doing a real work down there," LaMarcus said. "What we've been trying to do is get back to the roots. We don't care about denominational doctrine. We are only interested in reading the Bible and discovering from there how we are supposed to live and how God wants us to walk with him. When we dig that deep in an environment where we can discuss instead of just learn, well, you can see for yourself the fruits of what the Holy Spirit can do."

"I most certainly can," Pastor Mills agreed.

"The poorer communities of Mobile have gone through a great change. But I believe, sir, that the only way this change can last for decades and not just years is for the rest of the city to get on board; for the richer communities to meet with the poor. We would like to extend the offer for everyone else to join us. We would love to hold meetings in your communities, and we would love for all y'all to come to our community as well," LaMarcus said.

"That sounds like an amazing idea, LaMarcus," Pastor Mills said. "But how is it you think I can help?"

"I've also done my fair share of research, Pastor, and I know you have an influential voice on this side of the interstate, and it's growing. I think that you have a better chance of convincing others to join than I do. I've even listened to your preaching. It's bold. It's controversial, convicting even. It's what I love to see from a preacher and just from a man of God in general. It's how I teach and how I was taught to teach from both my mentor and by God. We have to try this somehow, Pastor. The one thing I see that our side of the interstate is succeeding at and yours is not, is rejecting the spirit of religion. These barriers are not easy to brake, but they have to be broken if God is to do the most for His people."

Pastor Mills was astonished by the wisdom coming from this young man. Truly, the favor of God was upon him. "I agree with you one-hundred percent, LaMarcus. I think this is what God is calling us to do."

"There is one other reason I want to do this, aside from it being good for the city," LaMarcus said. "I believe that soon, Satan will use his puppets to put together a plan to quench Jesus from our city altogether, making what I'm doing illegal and what you're doing illegal. If we can get these meetings established throughout Mobile, we may well be looking at the beginnings of the underground church."

"You are absolutely right. We'll need to get started right away." The pastor was getting excited now. "I'll make some calls to other churches and get the ball rolling. LaMarcus, if you wouldn't mind, I would like for you to preach in my church next Sunday. It can be on anything you want, but if I'm going to convince my congregation of anything, I think they need to know who you are. What do you say?"

"I'd be honored, sir," LaMarcus said, shaking Pastor Mills's hand.

LaMarcus's efforts were not in vain, either. He preached that next Sunday morning with pure, Holy Spirit fire. That church, who was used to hearing convicting sermons, was floored when they heard LaMarcus speak. LaMarcus shared his testimony with them and preached against the spirit of religion. Members of the congregation walked away in shock and awe at the work Jesus had done in this young man. It was exactly the catalyst that LaMarcus needed to get His plan going.

LaMarcus began getting calls from different churches, asking him to preach. Some of these churches were the most religious and bone-headedly doctrinal churches you could find, but God moved in the hearts of the pastors to allow LaMarcus to speak. There were different churches and church members who didn't like what LaMarcus said, and clung to their religious pride, but many who heard him speak were convicted of the importance of studying the Word themselves.

LaMarcus also took the time to detail the importance of preparing for suffering, which many of the religious church members didn't like. Any time he was confronted with the same old rhetoric of suffering, he would put them down, hard. It may have been strong words to use, but all LaMarcus was doing was telling the truth. The guilt and humiliation that the religious members would feel was all created by them.

The opposition outside the church was present as well. LaMarcus, his family, and his friends, all occasionally received death threats from Islamic activists, or from some people who just hated them and what they stood for. No one deterred in the slightest from the mission, even as the letters piled up. In fact, the letters only encouraged them to keep moving forward. A gang that at one time was dedicated to crime was now a group that was dedicated to the Lord, and no one was going to scare or intimidate them.

This sort of life continued for months. For LaMarcus and Tank especially, but also with the other three men, their fame on both sides of the aisle grew as they continued to walk where the Lord led them. Eventually, they were called even to preach in churches in other cities like Pensacola, Biloxi, Hattiesburg, and even as far north as Birmingham. For a group of guys who didn't have a lot of money, this was like travelling across the world.

About a year after LaMarcus was released from prison, plans were being made to hold a big event at the Mitchell Center, which was a big building on the campus of the University of South Alabama. It was used for all kinds of different events. Aside from being the location for the university's home games in both men and women's basketball, it was also used for most of the high school graduation ceremonies. Also, every year it held an event called Winter Jam, which was a concert tour of various Christian artists. So the Mitchell Center itself was not a stranger to holding Christian events in its walls.

Pastor Mills was friends with the mayor (not the same mayor who was in power during Mr. Curtis's satanic execution), and the two managed to convince the university president to let them hold this event on their grounds. The whole thing was very reminiscent of a Billy Graham preaching, only with a little more of a modern twist to it. For example, while LaMarcus certainly preached with the power of the Holy Spirit, he didn't have that instantly recognizable voice that Billy Graham had.

Also, there was the music. Billy Graham events played hymns like it was the only acceptable form of singing to God. As much as LaMarcus wanted to bring in his favorite Christian rapper, he thought it best to compromise and find an artist who could be appreciated by everyone. Pastor Mills had the perfect person in mind, and after playing many different songs, LaMarcus himself was convinced that this would be the best all-around person to bring in. He had varying styles, so he brought something for all demographics. Plus, he had an amazing testimony, and LaMarcus figured that if something happened to him, they could always let this guy speak. In short, the negotiations were made, and the city brought in this well respected Christian artist who drove to Mobile all the way from Muskogee, Oklahoma.

Extra security was brought in for the event. The mayor's desk was flooded daily with countless threats and tips of bomb threats at, and in response to, this event. State troopers were called in to give relief to the local police, but when the threats began to grow more, the governor caught wind and deployed a unit of the Alabama National Guard and ordered them to be on standby. It was clear that the powers of darkness did not want this event to happen. The mayor began to get shaky about the whole thing. He wanted it to happen but didn't want to put his citizens in danger. An uneasiness of doubt began to swirl in all of those that led the event.

LaMarcus prayed about what to do, and after long conversations with God, he called a meeting of all those who were working and volunteering the event, and those who were to be a part of it. They had to use the backstage area of the Mitchell Center where props were stored and the food was delivered to hold the meeting, for the number of volunteers and participants was sizeable in its own right.

"I'm going to make this short and sweet," LaMarcus told them. "I know we have people who want to see this whole thing shut down. They've threatened us. They've attacked us, and I know we've only begun to see the fury they possess. I also know that fear is amidst everyone in this room. If we were anybody else, they would be frightening. But we're not just anybody else. We are children of God. Don't be afraid of them. They say they'll come and kill us if we continue forward. I say, let them come. For even if we die, I say we show them the love of Christ and just exactly why we serve Jesus. Let us show them the power of the Living God. I ask you to stand with me, and stand firm in faith. Don't quit, and don't back down, because, why are we doing this? Not for ourselves, but for the glory of God. We are here to lift up the name of Jesus, a name that we are compelled to remain faithful to, because He is looking for a faithful people. So I'll ask you now the same question that Jesus asks of us: will you stand with me?"

When he was finished, a roar of cheers emerged from the crowd. LaMarcus turned to the mayor and said, "There's our answer to them. We let go and let God take over." The mayor shook his head in approval.

The volunteers worked like ants from that point forward. The assembly of the stage was in record time. The lighting, electronics, everything just seemed to fall into place. A special ramp was built in the back to bring the piano onto the stage for the music. Chairs lined the floor of the main arena just like the graduation ceremonies. Chairs were also set up on stage as well. They were reserved for the mayor and other city officials as well as for Pastor Mills, Jacoby, Thomas, Kelvin, and Tank. A podium was set front and center of the stage, and the grand piano was set to the right and a few feet back from the edge of the stage.

Cameras were set up so the event could be streamed and also recorded. It was a church service on steroids, just like what Billy Graham used to do. That having been said, it was a lot more humble of an event compared to other megachurch services, and contained more truth than those churches had ever shared in their entire existence. LaMarcus had resolved not to do an alter call. He never did when he preached. He explained to people that the decision to follow Jesus was the toughest and most personal decision you will ever make, and while public committals are nice, one-on-ones with Christ generally are the ones that are real. He explained that far too many people come up to the altar, say the prayer, and think they're saved. What makes the difference is the change in the heart. Two people can go to the altar, say the exact same prayer, and then leave, but only one would be saved and not the other. The difference was that one made a commitment, and the other was just going through the motions.

The day arrived and the hour was getting closer. Tank was looking for LaMarcus to take him to the stage and found him in the bathroom, throwing up.

Tank laughed at him and asked, "Are you nervous or something?"

LaMarcus looked up at him. "I've never preached to this many people at once before. I'm just...coping."

"Don't sweat it. You've done this a thousand times before, and God is with you," Tank reassured him.

"I know it," LaMarcus said. "We better get going."

With that, LaMarcus cleaned up, and they walked to another part of the backstage area and met up with everyone else, including the mayor. They all started walking to the stage together. LaMarcus had never been inside the main arena before, and he thought it was huge. Then he looked around and realized that it looked awfully familiar. In fact, he knew he had been here before and with this exact same setup too. It was the same stage, same lighting, same podium, and the same chairs. Only this time, as LaMarcus looked out from the stage, the chairs weren't empty, but rather they had people in them, and the number of empty seats was shrinking. LaMarcus grinned with that same feeling he had when he first got saved. *God really is amazing,* he thought to himself.

The worship music was incredible. For over an hour, song after song of love and intimacy with God was sung, and the service could have ended right there. But then it was time for LaMarcus to speak. He walked up to the podium, and the crowd eagerly awaited what he had to say. He took a deep breath.

"Revelation 12:11 says, 'And they overcame him by the blood of the Lamb and by the word of their testimony, and they loved not their lives even unto death.' Today, I will be preaching by the blood of the Lamb and by the word of my testimony."

www.ingramcontent.com/pod-product-compliance
Lightning Source LLC
Chambersburg PA
CBHW070813250626
47170CB00006B/2091